The Resident

Notorious ex-spy, womaniser and whisky lover George Mado is 'resting'. His extensive knowledge of Iron Curtain strengths and weaknesses, however, still carries weight at the top of the Service. Somewhat against his will, therefore, he finds himself catapulted from the deceptive calm of a Whitehall desk-job into the undergrowth of political intrigue, espionage and defection.

The scene is the Athens of the Colonels' outwardly peaceful regime. At the Russian Embassy, Alexei Voznitsky, the senior KGB officer, although a stern party-man, enjoys to the full his last posting to the cultured, degenerate West . . . Out on the coast, in his gorgeous white villa near Vouliagmeni, Panayotis Marides, dynamic multi-millionaire with a hoary peasant finger in every political pie, probes the enigma of his beautiful new wife, Elissa, widow of the arch defector, Paul Tarnham . . . In a small basement room of the Royal Greek Institute of Marine Research, the distinguished Russian oceanographer, Dr Petrov, makes love to his Greek secretary, Helen, who is Marides' niece . . . En route for the holidays from his English school, 15-year-old Mark Tarnham, Elissa's son, is diverted for an unexpected courtesy visit . . . An attractive but icy columnist from one of the British Sundays, Andrea Eckersley, arrives in Athens to cover the East European Trade Fair with totally unpredictable results . . .

In the heat of a glorious Greek summer, the sophisticated embassy life of a great and ancient capital rides uneasily on the knife-edge tensions of conflicting international self-interest. The story reaches a climax of terror and bloodshed in a hotel room in Athens where George Mado plays his highest card.

Also by Warren Tute

Novels
The Felthams (1950)
Lady in Thin Armour (1951)
Gentleman in Pink Uniform (1952)
The Younger Felthams (1953)
Girl in the Limelight (1954)
The Cruiser (1955)
The Rock (1957)
Leviathan (1959)
The Golden Greek (1960)
The Admiral (1963)
A Matter of Diplomacy (1969)
The Powder Train (1970)
The Tarnham Connection (1971)

History
The Grey Top Hat (1961)
Atlantic Conquest (1962)
Cochrane (1964)
Escape Route Green (1971)
The Deadly Stroke (1973)
Hitler: The Last Ten Days (1973)

Miscellaneous
Chico (1950)
Life of a circus bear (1952)
(with Felix Fonteyn) Cockney cats (1953)
Le Petomane (1967)

Plays
Jessica
A time to be born
A few days at Greece
Frost at midnight (translation)
Quartet for five (translation)

WARREN TUTE

The Resident

Constable London

First published in Great Britain 1973
by Constable & Company Ltd
10 Orange Street, London WC2H 7EG
Copyright © 1973 by Warren Tute

ISBN 0 09 459480 5

Set in Intertype Plantin
Printed in Great Britain by
The Anchor Press Ltd
and bound by
Wm. Brendon & Son Ltd
both of Tiptree, Essex

The Resident

I

It began in London. Now that George Mado had been reinstated in the Security Service – 'plugged in again' was how he put it himself – he had become a daily commuter to the dreary little Soho building, where his branch of the outfit currently worked. It was a desk job. He had always disliked the paperwork but it meant a regular salary and his pension was secure. As you neared sixty such considerations were important.

'I'm seeing Padstow today,' he told his wife in bed, after they had listened to the usual 7.00 a.m. roll-call of bombings in Ulster. He felt her instantly stiffen, but she made no reply.

'Just routine,' he added, caressing her breasts. He found he could never be completely convincing with Anna. She removed his hand from its investigating mission and turned away.

'Don't accept it. Say you won't go.'

'Accept what? And go where?'

'Don't play the innocent with me,' Anna said sharply, 'the deal was to work in an office – and take care of your wife and child.'

'And don't I?' he pleaded, beginning to make love to her. Having a child had seemed to increase her desirability. Unkind people might – and did – call her a meaty Czech dumpling: to Mado she exactly satisfied his sexual tastes and the marriage was a success on that basis alone. But now her Middle European instincts scented danger. She was not going to be fobbed off with an early morning session.

'I don't trust that young man,' she said.

'Well, I do.'

'You promised, George. You promised you wouldn't do any more field work.'

There was a catch in her voice which moved him. It had been a new experience to George Mado at his stage in life to have an attractive young woman who actually liked him for himself, who genuinely cared about what might happen to him. Someone who knew and assessed the dangers, and who had wanted his child.

'Look, my darling, let's keep things on the ground. I've no idea why young Mr Padstow wants to see me today but you know and I know and he knows, too, that the chances of my being the slightest use in the role I once played are nil. Zero. Absolute zero. The espionage services of every country in the world have George Mado on file as a blown spy – blown as high as the dome of St Peter's. So the days of secret missions are over. They all recognise who I am and what I get up to.'

'Well, you're not getting up me,' Anna said curtly, pushing him away, 'I can make conditions, too.'

'You Czechs can be very vulgar at times. If this goes on, I might have just cause and reason to be unfaithful – sexually that is.'

'Don't make me laugh,' Anna said, getting out of bed and tantalising him even further with her ripe nakedness. 'If I turn my back for two seconds, you're having it off with the nearest au pair you can manage to chat up.'

'Sometimes I like it better when you turn your back,' Mado said and took her as she bent down to put on her bedroom slippers. In the next room their infant daughter began to yowl for her morning feed.

Of course Anna's hunches had usually proved to be right, Mado thought, as he walked lunchwards to Pall Mall. His morning's office work had not strained his intelligence, and he had had plenty of time to think. An intuitive man himself, Mado had not reached his present age without acquiring a high respect for the instinct of others. He was also aware of the operation of 'those things unseen' of which, so the Bible said, 'faith was the evidence'.

It was a fine July day, sunny but not too hot. London had already begun absorbing into itself that tide of students, bearded, bra-less or unisexed, which Mado found more and more stimulating as the years went by. Eroticism, and every level of sexual response, had always loomed large in Mado's life. He loved women and women in fair numbers had loved him.

So such a walk on such a clear, balmy day with the smiles he gave and received from those tall, nubile girls outside American Express, should normally have filled him with contentment. Instead, as he neared the august establishment club to which young Mr Padstow had bidden him, his sense of unease grew until it was actually bobbing about in his conscious mind.

'Anna says I'm not to agree,' he remarked, once they had got over the preliminaries, 'the deal was a desk job and I'm to look after my wife and child.'

'She's a great girl, your Anna,' John Padstow said with one of his sideways smiles, 'but for once she's got it all wrong. I just wanted to have you to lunch and see how you were after – how long is it now? A year? You know me, George, there's nothing devious in me.'

Mado laughed into his Scotch.

'When I think back to Beirut . . . and the help you were to me on Operation Powder Train . . .'

'You're not supposed to jeer openly at your host in a

9

club of this kind. Things have changed since we terminated the Tarnham connection.'

Mado looked out of the window into the dark little garden at the back of Pall Mall into which nobody ever went. He had had to change his mind about young Mr Padstow, who was now very high up in the outfit indeed. He had once thought him as wet as a scrubber, but Padstow had proved himself in the two previous operations and willy-nilly Mado had come to like and respect him. Of course he also had the right connections, a factor conspicuously missing from Mado's life.

'I must say I never thought you of all people would end up as a pillar of Establishment . . . and my boss into the bargain.'

'And *I* never thought they'd let *you* back in,' Padstow countered drily, 'knowing Whitehall as I now do. But here we both are.'

Mado directed on him one of his hard, calculating looks.

'Come on, sport, I'd like to enjoy this expensive lunch, so tell me what it's all about.'

'Very well. I do have a job I want you to do, but it isn't specific.'

'That tells me nothing at all. Where would it be?'

'Greece.'

Mado screwed up his puggy face into what he imagined to be a Middle Eastern expression of distaste.

'Not Marides and Elissa all over again? I thought those two were on an even keel at last.'

'They come into it,' Padstow said, 'but only indirectly – at least as I see it at present.'

'A multi-millionaire of Panayotis Marides' power comes into everything in Greece. But I thought he was turning his attention to China?'

'He is.'

'It gets him away from Elissa, I suppose.'

'Now come on, George, I know you've never liked her but Tarnham is good and dead, and she did marry Marides.'

'She's still the mother of Tarnham's children, who are very much alive.'

'Yes,' Padstow agreed, 'and that's something else. The boy's a problem in his own. The girl goes to an English school in Athens but young Master Mark is at a public school here in England. He flies out to Greece for the holidays.'

'That must please Panayotis. He once told me he thought of pushing them off his yacht on a dark night. He's quite capable of that sort of mayhem when he gets in a nasty mood.'

'Well nowadays – surprising as it may seem to you, George – Madame has things much her own way. Once Marides persuaded her to marry him, he thought his troubles were over. My guess is they've only just begun.'

Mado went back in his mind over the many complicated events of the previous seven years from Paul Tarnham's defection to his death in Czechoslovakia. Since the scene was again going to be Greece, he excavated his memories of Elissa's first visit to Athens when a serious matter of diplomacy had been involved and an attempt to suborn the Counsellor of the British Embassy had been executed by Tarnham himself. The children had always been well placed pawns in the game.

'The boy wanted to follow his father to Russia,' Mado observed, 'and I used to think the sooner he did so the better for all concerned. Mark Tarnham was very much his father's boy.'

'He still is,' Padstow said, 'and the KGB consider he's ripe for recruitment, even at the age of fifteen. But that's not why I asked you here today. The Greeks have organised a Trade Fair – an Eastern European Trade Fair in Athens and up north in Salonika.'

'Those Colonels are really living it up.'

'It proves how liberal they are.'

'Look, sport, I don't know what you're going to ask me to do, but I don't have to tell you I can't exactly operate as a secret agent any more. One or two people do identify my squashed-in nose. Some of them even remember how it came to be broken. They can also recall my name.'

'Exactly. And that's why I want you in Greece. I'll get you a diplomatic passport and some sort of useless job in the commercial section of the Embassy.'

'Why?'

'Simply because everyone *does* know who you are. The Embassy may not like it very much but you'll act as a sort of magnet. You'll go to all the parties. You'll be out there in front.'

'A sort of stool-pigeon, you mean?'

'No one's going to take a pot shot at you, George. Not nowadays – not in Greece. Your very notoriety protects you. But the point is you're available. You can be trusted, you're there to be consulted should . . . should anyone feel like asking your advice.'

'I see. You think someone's ripe to do a reverse Tarnham, in effect?'

'Possibly. Someone is certainly in love with his secretary. You know how Russians are when sex gets into the act.'

'I know how most of us are, so far as that side of things is concerned.'

'Yes, well this one is an oceanographer and marine biologist with an international reputation.'

'I shouldn't have thought there was much of a defence element in that.'

'The Russian Navy wouldn't agree, George. They think he's very precious indeed.'

'And he's having it off with his secretary? Tch! tch! tch!'

'His Greek secretary – and a cousin of Panayotis Marides. I'm not sure she isn't a niece. Anyway she was born in the same village in the Pindus mountains.'

'It's an unlikely combination,' Mado said, thinking it out, 'how does he come to have a Greek secretary at all? And who is he when he's at home?'

'Dr Sergei Vassilievitch Petrov.'

'I wonder what she calls him in bed.'

Padstow gave him the sort of look a General might give a rather tiresome ADC.

'Do you ever think about anything else than sex? As a matter of fact she calls him Smootchi.'

'Oh dear!'

'Yes. It's the full sentimental bit, I'm afraid. They met at UNESCO in Paris – that Piccadilly Circus of espionage.' The upper-class disdain in Padstow's voice caused Mado to smile to himself. 'Her name is Helen Stanopoulos and she's more of a personal assistant than a secretary. She's university trained and the Russians offered her a job helping Petrov to organise the scientific section of the East European Trade Fair. They pay her well – Petrov sees to that – and everything in the garden is lovely. Only . . .' Padstow paused and shot Mado a sharp look, 'when the exhibition is over, Dr Petrov returns to Russia where his wife and family, of course, remain.'

'I see.'

For a while neither spoke. Both men tucked into the expensive meal young Mr Padstow would charge up to the firm and considered the implications from their respective points of view. At last Mado broke the silence.

'You don't need me for a possibility of that kind.' He shrugged his shoulders. 'So a Russian wants to defect – he picks his moment when the guardian apes aren't around and defects.'

'He's in Greece, George. He doesn't speak Greek.'

'I'll bet he's learnt the essentials.'

'Do you know what happened here in London to the last one who made the break? He picked on a traffic warden and addressed her in Russian.'

'That must have made her day.'

'She was writing out a ticket for a parking offence. She said she was busy and to ask someone else. Then the apes, as you call them, caught up and started to drag him away to a car.'

'Things are getting rough these days in our clean London streets. What happened?'

'The traffic warden wasn't going to have that sort of thing on her beat. So when they'd forced him into the car, she got a laundry van to block it in and then whistled up the police. But it was a near thing. Once that car had got back to Kensington Palace Gardens, it would have been Ivan's last farewell.'

'Yes,' Mado murmured, thinking back to his two experiences of the Lubyanka prison in Moscow, 'I know about that side of things.'

'Of course Dr Petrov may simply go back to the USSR nursing his bruised heart.'

'But you think it's worth the expense of sending good old reliable Mado to case up the scene in Greece? Just on the chance? I don't believe it.' Then a sudden idea struck him. 'Who's the Resident in Greece?'

'Ah! yes,' said Padstow, ordering brandy and cigars, 'I see you haven't lost your touch. I'll tell you about him in a moment or so. I think *he* may be interested in Elissa.'

'The Resident' is the senior KGB officer in any given territory. He is never the Ambassador and usually not even apparently a senior Embassy official. Inside the Russian Embassy, however, whether in New York or Kampala, everyone knows who he is. He may nominally hold down some minor post on the commercial or cultural side. This will enable him to move about the country on legitimate Embassy business and to receive each and every kind of visitor without attracting undue attention from the security services of the country concerned.

In fact he is simply the King of Spies in that particular area and he keeps an intense watch not only on his host country but also on his own staff and on the staffs of all other embassies of the communist bloc. Inevitably his power is immense since he is the one man in that area whom Moscow trusts. No one on the spot has direct control of the Resident unless and until things go wrong. Then and only then, in the manner of the medieval Roman Catholic Church, an inquisitor with plenary powers is sent.

Alexei Voznitsky, the Resident in Athens, was fully and intelligently aware of his position and of the power he enjoyed. Forty-seven years old, he had been born nearly a decade after the October Revolution. His aristocratic grandfather had been an officer in the Imperial Army of the Czar but had had the wisdom to get himself killed in obscure circumstances in 1917. By dint of a change of name and some clever footwork on the part of his father who had grasped the realities of the situation sooner than his contemporaries, the young Voznitsky had succeeded not only in staying alive through the Stalin era – a feat in itself – but also in securing a commission in Beria's outfit which later became the KGB, perhaps the most powerful private army in the history of the world. Now in Athens he was enjoying his local Czardom to the full.

'I have invited Dr Petrov and his secretary to dinner tonight,' his wife said at breakfast, 'I tried to contact you yesterday but you were out all day.'

'And I suppose you know where,' Voznitsky replied with a slight edge to his voice. He might be the local Commissar but standard KGB practice ensured that his wife kept a silent and independent watch on him as a counter-check.

'Well, Alexei, is it convenient or not?'

He nodded but exhibited no pleasure. He had been looking forward to a quiet evening at home drinking French wine and listening to an opera on his stereo equipment.

'Will you cook for them here or shall I get a table at the Karamaikis?'

Irina shrugged her shoulders.

'I don't particularly like Dr Petrov or his girl-friend,' she said, 'so unless you want to talk to him in private I'd rather not bother to have them here to dinner.'

'I'm scarcely likely to talk to Petrov in private if his girl-friend is present,' Voznitsky retorted. He was fond of his wife but for someone who also had a commission in the KGB she could be at times almost intentionally stupid and obtuse. Of course it was the little boy who worried Irina.

'But she is his personal assistant and they are sleeping together.'

'The girl is Greek,' Voznitsky said severely, 'if she had been a Russian from the Embassy staff that might be different. But no – he has to pick on a Greek. Our famous Dr Petrov may know a great deal about plankton and algae, he doesn't seem to be very aware of the world he lives in.'

'But he's loyal, isn't he, Alexei?'

There was an anxious tone in her voice. Voznitsky knew she didn't care a hoot about Petrov or his loyalty. She was thinking of Petrov's wife and family now being casually deceived, and therefore at risk. Her own little son, whom they had had to leave behind in Moscow with her mother, was also never for long out of her thoughts. Voznitsky was suddenly touched by the look on her face.

'You're pining for Boris, aren't you?' Voznitsky said. No one could describe Irina as beautiful but she had the normal attractiveness of a healthy young mother, to which was now added the melancholy sadness of having to be parted from their only child. At seven Boris was being forced to learn the hard facts of Russian soviet life. He had been forbidden to go abroad with his distinguished parents. He had to remain with his maternal grandmother under the watchful eye of the KGB. What made it worse was that Irina had never got on with her mother, whom she thought of as a secret church-going counter-revolutionary. It was therefore doubly depressing to have to leave Boris in her care whilst she and Alexei were on this foreign assignment.

'Of course I miss him,' she snapped, 'that's all I have, isn't it?'

'I don't know what you mean,' Voznitsky said defensively, knowing full well what she was implying.

'You men seize the first opportunity you can grab of having an affair. You go off abroad, you seduce your secretaries or your cypher clerks, anyone dazzled by your rank and your power and you leave us women to carry the whole burden of the family on our own. I wonder what Mrs Petrov thinks of it all.'

'Us women!' Voznitsky said contemptuously, 'always these clichés. I suppose you'll be taking Women's Lib back to Moscow with one or two other bourgeois ideas.'

'Why don't you go to your office?' she said, 'I have to superintend the cleaning of this apartment.'

It always ended like that, Voznitsky thought, as he drove to the Embassy. Communication grew less and less as time

17

went by. To begin with you were in love and you sated yourself with sex. It was all a trick, an illusion. Then came the payment, the responsibilities of family, the gradual drawing apart. Yet always you were caught. If he had not been married, if he had not been able to offer a hostage in the form of a seven-year-old, much loved son, he would never have been allowed to come abroad holding the high rank he did in the KGB.

Not that he argued with this. Some such system was essential and he accepted it. He hated capitalism. Foreign service in the KGB was looked on Jesuitically as the front line of the war which communism eternally waged on the capitalist world. Voznitsky fully concurred in this. He had an utter contempt for someone like Marides, a capitalist of capitalists, a monster of Western decadence.

Nevertheless some of the restrictions were hard to bear. Voznitsky's very success had enabled him to acquire expensive tastes in wine, music and Western literature – in all of which he was free to indulge to any degree he chose, since locally there was no one to say him nay.

Equally, of course, there was no one with whom he could share these tastes. Perhaps it was his aristocratic grandfather's spirit still latent in him which gave him such a disdain of his brother officers in the KGB. Almost without exception they had the civilisation of the higher apes. They drank, they rutted away at sex, they played sentimental Russian music and they lived, so it seemed to Voznitsky, almost entirely in and for their bodies.

You discussed culture, if at all, as a duty and you dealt with it in quantities, assuming that the more you took in the more educated you were. It did not matter if the art you absorbed had no meaning. Life itself had no meaning to his brother officers of the KGB except on a physical and lower mental plane. Understanding – the possibility of a soul –

18

these were non-Marxist concepts to be treated with the contempt they deserved. It was unfortunate, therefore, that Voznitsky happened to believe that the soul existed. No one had asked him about God for many years but Voznitsky was aware of his presence too. This was not altogether a happy situation for a senior officer such as himself.

Out on the coast near Vouliagmeni, the great white house, covered with purple Bougainvillaea, which Panayotis Marides had built as his main palace in Greece, had by now been gradually transformed into a home. 'Humanised,' was the word Elissa used to herself. She had come through some sort of sound barrier and was enjoying her marriage and the new life which her Greek millionaire husband took such pleasure in giving her.

'And next, I suppose, it will be a family,' Marides said, half-serious, half-aggressive in that stubborn peasant manner he always fell back on when in doubt. He was one of the richest men in the world but his roots, in spite of the British nationality he had acquired via Cyprus in the colonial days, were still firmly in the Pindus mountains of north-west Greece.

'I think that decision has already been taken,' Elissa answered, 'but I'll let you know for certain when you come back from Pekin.'

They were having a late morning ouzo on the terrace overlooking the private beach. For once no guests were expected for lunch and they had no one staying in the house.

'You're joking,' Marides said quietly, but with a hesitancy in the voice which would have been imperceptible to anyone except Elissa. He did not know how to take this news, so he probed and hedged. She studied his swarthy, intelligent face. A few years ago when the well-bred, ascetic-looking Paul Tarnham had dominated her life, it was unthinkable even to consider an intimate life with such a man as Marides. Yet here she was now, not only agreeably married to him but also pregnant, as she now felt reasonably certain.

'You didn't think I married you for your collection of Impressionists, did you?'

'No, but I mean – are you serious or not?'

'Don't you want another son?'

'It needs thinking about. I have a son already.'

'Yes,' Elissa said grittily, 'and so far as I am concerned, you can keep him.'

'He's a good boy,' Marides said defensively.

'Some boy!'

She jeered, but not in such an unkind way that Marides could really take offence. She had learnt always to talk so that her husband never knew if she fully meant what she said. Half truths were very much in the Greek tradition.

'He'd slit your throat if he thought he could get away with it. And he'd certainly dispose of me if he could.'

'Yach!' said Marides, who hated direct statements of that kind, 'I'm not so sure about your own son by Tarnham.'

'My own son by Tarnham, as you put it, is not quite in the same position to slit throats as your Christos. He's only fifteen. And he doesn't work in the Greek Foreign Office.'

'He's learning fast.'

'How do you know?'

Marides smiled, drawing back his head slightly and half-closing his eyes in that peculiarly Greek way of showing contempt. He gave his wife what a Victorian novelist would call 'a veiled look'. Then he shrugged his shoulders, and dropped into the Greek-American accent which he knew irritated her.

'I don't-a know a thing. He's-a your son. You know him

best. You have him expensively educated in England. But I tell you – he's more his father's son than yours.'

'What do you mean by that?'

'Problems,' Marides said enigmatically, 'always a boy like that brings problems.'

'You've been talking to your Russian friends again.'

'And what's wrong with that? They charter my ships.'

'You know what I mean. That Voznitsky.'

'No, Elissa, I don't know what you mean.' There was no one better at turning a question or dodging an issue when he chose than Marides.

'But as we're talking about my Russian friends,' he went on, 'I'd be grateful if you'd keep an eye on Helen whilst I'm away. I'm not sure Dr Petrov knows what he's doing.'

'Then it's a little late, isn't it?' Elissa said crisply. 'What sort of an eye am I to keep? Is she pregnant too?'

'I hope not. Her father would wring her neck like a chicken.'

'You're so dramatic, you Greeks. What's it matter if she loves him?'

'It matters in a Greek village. Petrov has a wife and family in Russia.' He gave her an irritated look. 'I don't think you'd better go to the Pindus mountains with ideas like that. Even as my wife. They might stone you.'

She went over and put an arm round his shoulder.

'I was only joking,' she said, 'I'd forgotten the Greek mafia. I'll do what I can for Helen, but she's a headstrong girl. She's a little like you.'

'Not – very like me,' Marides said with a frown, 'not if she makes a fool of herself with that dumb Russian scientist.'

It was a small, hot room in the basement, not over clean, and outside stood the dustbins of the Royal Greek Institute of Marine Research. It was the caretaker's place and as such would not have unduly shamed a French *concierge* in a working-class district. But it was airless, especially when the curtains were drawn, and not exactly the most romantic setting for a love affair.

Anyone lying on her back, as Helen was now doing with the momentarily relaxed bulk of her beloved Smootchi on top of her, could watch the cockroaches bustling about the ceiling and occasionally falling off on to the bed. It was far from perfect. But it was all they could get. Its location provided a waterproof alibi since it was legitimate for Dr Petrov to spend as much time as he deemed necessary in the Institute where the Greek authorities had given him an office and where in turn he had installed his personal assistant. The fact that they were so rarely in the office itself aroused no comment since there were always conferences to be attended elsewhere in the building and valuable Aegean records to be studied in the vaults, amongst other places, next to the caretaker's room.

Helen had bribed the caretaker with surprisingly little difficulty. She was also under the impression that their basement *garconnière* was known only to themselves. The caretaker had been at the Institute for years. He was a wizened, grey-haired old man with blackened teeth from the tobacco he chewed rather than smoked. He lived for the lottery and any spare drachma he acquired went straight into lottery tickets. He was a typical, uncomplicated Greek watchman. The Police, of course, had him where they wanted him and, if they asked questions, would undoubtedly get everything he knew or suspected.

But what, after all, did he know? That one of the Professors wanted to have an affair with his secretary? Well, that had happened before. Nothing unusual in that. The caretaker kept out of the way, except when he felt that another tip was due. And it never occurred to either Helen Stanopoulos or Dr Sergei Petrov to look under the bed, where the Greek security forces had placed a small Japanese tape recorder; nor to examine the lapels of Dr Petrov's suit, where a pinhead microphone had been put by the Russians which picked up everything within a radius of ten metres and transmitted it to a car with CD plates outside the institute, where the love chatter emitted by two people in sexual congress was automatically and blindly recorded for possible future use.

Suddenly Petrov raised himself on his elbows and looked down on her face.

'Why are you crying?' he asked. 'Is there something wrong?'

Their common language was French since Helen spoke no Russian and Petrov only enough Greek to order a restaurant meal. Moreover they had met in Paris so French became naturally their language of love.

'I want it to go on for ever,' she said, 'and it won't.'

She turned her head as the tears poured down on to the grimy pillow. She was small and dark, with big expressive brown eyes and delicate hands. It did not seem to matter that Petrov was at least twenty-three years older than she was. She did not mind his middle-aged paunch, nor his thinning hair. In her eyes he was a highly intelligent, highly qualified man and she loved him. They separated their bodies and he traced away the tears with his finger.

'Don't cry,' he said, 'I don't like it when you cry. I love you, little Helen.'

'That's what you say. But you'll go back to Russia, to your wife and family, and forget all about me.'

It was true but he hated her saying it.

'Yes,' he said at last, 'I do have to go back. But I shan't forget about you.'

23

'That won't do me much good,' Helen said, getting out of bed and beginning to dress, 'I'll be here and you'll be there.'

'Then why don't you come with me? I'll get a divorce and we'll marry. Then we could go on working together . . .'

He faltered into silence. Like Helen he wanted it to go on for ever and like her also knew that it wouldn't. He was an autocratic man by nature and resented finding himself in his present weak position.

'I don't think that's a very proper idea,' she said, tossing her head and becoming once more the brisk, business-like secretary she had taught herself to appear. 'I'd better get back to the office, before people start wondering where we are. Call in on Records on your way back as that's where I shall say you've been if anyone asks.'

2

The Greek Trade Fair was scheduled to open early in August. This boosted the normal flow of summer tourists to Athens and overloaded travel and accommodation facilities. Even by using Marides' own airline, which went against Mado's grain since it meant more profit to someone already impossibly rich, the office could not get him the direct flight to Athens which he had wanted. Instead he was forced to change aircraft in Rome.

As he went through the departure lounge at Heathrow, however, Mado suspected that there may have been less accident than intent in this arrangement. Just ahead of him in the line of passengers boarding the aircraft was young Mark Tarnham, presumably en route to Athens for his holidays. Keeping close to the boy in that professional way Mado instantly recognised stood a tall, hard-looking man whose face was vaguely familiar to Mado although the identity escaped him.

This man and young Tarnham had not apparently made each other's acquaintance but, as if by chance, the man eased into the next seat to Mark, who was on the window side, the third seat being taken by a girl with high cheekbones and striking red hair, who was also known to Mado but whom for the moment he could not place.

Mado's years of experience had given him a chameleon quality which was invaluable. He could move fast and get where he needed to be without drawing attention to himself.

He used this now, charming an elderly American widow out of the way, to secure the aisle seat in the row behind. This enabled him to keep an eye on Mr Hatchet Face and the defector's son, although he could not hear what they might say to each other.

He also had the pleasure of studying the mop of wind-swept tawny hair in front of him and of wondering what the owner of the hair would be like. Rather hard and purposeful, he concluded. Tarnham's son, whom he had helped rescue from Prague in 1968, would certainly recognise him if he turned round but Mark seemed to be more of a moody introvert than ever. He at once immersed himself in a book, not even looking up when the aircraft took off.

This gave Mado more time to study the redhead in front of him, and eventually realise her identity. When they got off the plane at Rome, she was joined by a bearded young man with square metal-framed glasses and one of those student caps that made him look like a fugitive from *Dr Zhivago*. He was also carrying a disguised camera case and this signalled to Mado that he belonged to the current crop of press photographers.

'You're Andrea Eckersley, aren't you?' Mado said to the girl. He had still managed to remain unobserved by Mark Tarnham, now at the end of the transit lounge. The tall sinister man had disappeared.

'Thank you,' Andrea said coolly. She gave Mado a penetrating, keep-away look as if he were some square at a party who might ask her what sort of stuff she wrote.

'On holiday?'

'No,' Andrea said, again without warmth, 'my paper is sending us to cover the Trade Fair in Athens.'

'Ah!' said Mado, still keeping an eye on Mark Tarnham, 'I enjoy reading your column.'

'But . . . ?'

'No "buts" at all. You make me laugh. You've a very sharp eye.'

'Well, thank you again. This is Don Dowdall,' she flashed Mado a quick glint, 'whose photography you also admire.'

They nodded at each other.

'And who are you?' Andrea Eckersley enquired in a casual way. He wondered if she really knew or was simply trying him out.

'I'm George Smith, alias Brown. Sometimes known as Robinson.'

'Ah!' Andrea said, reacting with the sort of look a tart gives a difficult customer, 'you mean I ought to know who you are.'

'Not at all. My real name is Mado and I can't tell you how pleasant it is not to be recognised for a change. Especially by a lady and gent from the Press.'

'You're George Mado?' she said, and allowed the hard features to break into a smile, 'Well, well, well. That's made my day.'

'You could make mine,' Mado said with a smile.

'Could I indeed?'

'I'm a pretty coarse fellow under this well-bred, elegant exterior.'

'Oh!' she said, in her own unmistakably upper-class voice which she had tried for so long to disguise for Fleet Street purposes, 'so that's what you are . . .'

'People's ideas of breeding vary, don't they?' Mado chatted on.

'I know they breed rats for laboratory purposes.'

'Rats indeed!' Mado said, looking at her with an ironic smile, 'you can get very friendly with a rat. Especially if you meet in the right circumstances. Like a Russian prison, for instance. Rats rate above gaolers for me. But I was forget-

27

ting . . . you're a Marxist, aren't you, under that fair beautiful skin.'

'Never mind what I am,' Andrea snapped, 'I may need your help in Greece.'

'How did you know I was going to Greece?'

'I didn't. However, I just found out.'

'Where are you staying?'

'Intermittently at the Grande Bretagne. The paper likes it that way.'

He drew her slightly away from the photographer who, in any case, seemed to be absorbed by a passing Tarzan in airline uniform.

'How about standing me dinner tonight?' Mado suggested, 'I think your paper would like that, too. Or are you committed to Mr Dowdall?'

'Only for work purposes,' Andrea said with a slightly bleary expression, 'the ladies don't interest him very much.'

'Capital! Capital!' Mado went on, opting for his Edwardian *Forsyte Saga* mood, which she at once cut short.

'And you don't interest me, Mr Mado. At least not as a guest on my expense account.'

He smiled her a winning smile.

'We'll go Dutch.'

She smiled him back an equally charming negative.

'Oh! no, we won't.'

'All right,' he conceded the game, 'but don't eat too much. I work for the Government now.'

'Didn't you always?'

He looked at her and raised his eyebrows.

'I think we've a lot of finding out about each other to do.'

'Don't build up any hopes,' she said, 'I'm not that easy to know.' Then, quickly switching the subject, she went on: 'You've had to do with the Marides, haven't you?'

'Do you mean Panayotis, his Foreign Office son or his famous wife?'

'All three.'

'Yes,' Mado agreed, lighting a cigarette, 'I know the Marides. And if you look over my left shoulder in the corner by the poster advertising Sorrento, you can see Elissa's son by the late and unlamented Tarnham.'

'Oh yes?' Andrea said, 'the one with the straw hat – or the bearded old man in a skull cap?'

Mado whipped round and stared. Mark Tarnham was no longer visible in the transit lounge. He swore softly to himself and set off for the exit.

'But don't forget me,' Mado called over his shoulder as he went, 'I'll be back.'

He checked behind all the pillars. He checked the lavatories. Mark Tarnham had definitely gone and there was no trace either of the stony-faced man who had sat next to him in the aircraft. For some reason no official appeared to be in charge of the transit passengers at that time. So Mado did a quick tour of the airline desks and of the arrival and departure lounges. But Ciampino is a large airport. It was full of summer crowds. The search was doomed. Mado decided he might as well be looking for someone in Oxford Street on a Saturday morning.

In any event Mark Tarnham was only of oblique interest. If the boy wanted to follow in his father's footsteps, that was all right by Mado. Let him get on with it. He returned to the transit lounge to find that his plane for Athens had already left. It was not an auspicious start to his new assignment.

Andrea Eckersley had only admitted to part of the truth when she had told Mado that she and Don Dowdall had been sent to Athens for the East European Trade Fair.

This was her cover plan. In fact she had sold her editor the idea of a series of features on the world's richest men, and she intended to start on Panayotis Marides. Her regular column was being rested. She had worked hard for three years. There was every justification to give herself a break. Moreover, oddly enough, she had never visited Greece before.

She was an arresting-looking young woman with a determined, squarish jaw, blue eyes and that clear red hair which to Mado's surprise so often went with sexual frigidity. She looked, at first sight, like the sex symbol of all time with her slender body, well-defined waist and firm breasts. Strong white teeth, lyrical legs and thighs and that astonishing colouring – Mado had taken in all those plus factors – but experience and instinct combined to warn him that the more ravishing such a woman appeared, the less likely she was to be good in bed. It had all gone into the looks.

This was indeed the case with Andrea, who had never had a satisfactory love affair in her life. Moreover since most men reacted instantly and predictably to her attractiveness and then bent their best endeavours into getting her horizontal, she had developed a kind of brittle cynicism about the whole process. She certainly knew what to expect in France and Italy and she had no notion but that Greece would prove to be, if anything, even more exhausting.

Andrea had a further disability which she kept very quiet about in Fleet Street. She was an Earl's daughter. Being a Lady in her own right was less than no use to her in the competitive world she had chosen to enter. So when, on leaving Oxford, she had taken up with the writing, she had adopted her mother's name and had contrived, by keeping her home background and her working life completely separate, to make herself a reputation as a competent

30

journeyman writer with the full quota of left-wing bias acceptable to her brother and sister journalists who daily sold their souls to the capitalist press. At least this was the face she showed to the world. It was also the extent of Mado's knowledge of her.

What Mado did not know was that Andrea had agreed to work in a very discreet way for John Padstow, whom she had met and liked during an off-duty weekend at her parents' house in Dorset. Padstow had taken a risk in talking to her as he had. British security was well aware of Miss Eckersley's Maoist ideas but in spite of them she was no tatty little King Street traitor. She was loyal – if not to her Queen and country – at least to her ideas of English civilisation, freedom and to the general way of life which her socialist friends seemed so anxious to modify and even destroy without apparently realising what they were really doing. She was thus a paradox to herself and, had the orthodox communists known it, something of an enigma in reverse as Philby had been.

Padstow had not told Mado anything about her at all. In fact Andrea knew considerably more about Mado than she had given away on their first encounter. She had recognised him long before he had worked out who she was. It had also been no accident that she had sat next to young Mark Tarnham in the aircraft. She had been well briefed by Padstow before setting out and she carried a very private and personal letter of introduction from him to Elissa. She also had a more formal letter from her editor to Marides. All of this she kept to herself when eventually she and Mado met up in Athens.

'You're a little late,' she remarked as they greeted each other in the bar of the Grande Bretagne Hotel. 'Forty-eight hours late to be precise.'

31

'I'm sorry,' Mado said, 'I should learn not to chase hares at my time of life.'

'Did you track the boy down?'

'No, and I've been at the Embassy since I arrived so I haven't checked with Elissa yet. For all I know they may have meant him to get off that plane in Rome.'

'They did not. They expected him on the same flight we arrived on – or rather that I arrived on and that you should have caught.'

'You know the Marides already? I thought you were asking me for an introduction.'

'My editor gave me a letter to Marides about the series I hope to do.'

She told him about the features she intended to write. This satisfied Mado's curiosity. It was a part of her job. She made no mention of Padstow nor of the letter she had passed on to Elissa.

'You certainly don't waste time,' Mado said, giving her an appraising look, 'how was the great man when you met him?'

'Angry. They were together when I was ushered in. To begin with I pretended I didn't know about Mark being on the same plane, but it was one of the first questions Elissa asked me . . . "If you were on Alitalia XYZ or whatever – did you notice a young man etc etc etc?" I said I sat next to him. "Where is he then?" Marides said sourly, "he should have come on to Athens on the same plane as you." Then he turned to Elissa and said something about "This is becoming a habit." At which point she got angry, too.'

'You seem to have plunged to the heart of things in record time,' Mado said, studying her face with genuine admiration. 'You're quite a girl, aren't you? We should be a team.'

She laughed.

'You like to turn everything to your immediate advantage, don't you?' she said. 'What sort of team? And for what?'

One thing was clear to Mado. Andrea Eckersley would be no easy lay.

'Well, all right,' he said, 'the way things are shaping up we'll be working together, whether we like it or not.'

'Why?'

He wondered why a sudden flash of danger seemed to light up her eyes.

'Because you've evidently got a strong sense of news.' He paused, wondering how to take it on from there, 'and I suppose I have as well.'

She gave him a steady look and smiled.

'Why have you come to Athens?'

He allowed himself the sort of mocking smile she had turned on him when first they had met.

'For the East European Trade Fair.'

'I didn't know you were interested in commerce.'

'Young lady, I used to travel in books.' A somewhat puzzled look crossed her face so he went on, 'I'd have you know that you're speaking to a properly accredited Assistant Commercial Attaché at the British Embassy in Athens.'

She could look astonishingly innocent when she chose. She was what would have been called 'scrumptious' in Mado's youth. As if reading his thoughts, she put him down with a jolt by continuing what he had just said: 'Who has an attractive young wife, a small baby and a disgustingly roving eye.'

'What's disgusting about it?'

'Has no one ever told you?'

'As a matter of fact they haven't. At least no one's complained so far.'

'Well,' Andrea said crisply, 'you may have a super under-

33   T.R.—B

standing with your wife. I doubt you're going to have one with me.'

Such understanding as there was between Elissa and Panayotis had also been stretched to near breaking point by Mark's disappearance. Elissa had wanted to go straight to the British Embassy, but Marides had better ways of finding out what had happened and ordered her to keep the matter entirely to herself. Marides had spent the last few days in a sulky bad temper since the boy's disappearance. From his point of view it was a complication he could well have done without on the eve of an important visit to Pekin and the opening of the Trade Fair in Athens, where he intended to mature a number of tricky deals.

To celebrate this inauguration, he had arranged one of 'those sumptuous eighteenth-century extravaganzas' for some three hundred important guests – or at least guests who had some claim to importance – at the villa with its peerless view over the Aegean, where enough food and drink to keep Bangladesh going for a month would be consumed and which was to culminate in a firework display from the little island off the coast, which he also owned.

Elissa detested these exhibitions of wealth and power, but as they were an essential part of the man she loved and had married, she put up with them in such a way that Panayotis had no idea of her real feelings but thought she actually enjoyed them. In a sense this was true, since Elissa was aware of the almost childish delight it gave him and relished this pleasure, so to speak, at one remove. Privately she was appalled at the vulgarity of it all.

About an hour before the first guests were due to arrive, Marides arrived back in a rage.

'Your son by Tarnham,' he said, waving a letter in his hand, 'is in Moscow.'

Elissa froze rigid. She felt a tightening of the solar plexus and the onset of a fear she thought she would never have to experience again.

'How do you know?'

'Voznitsky. He gave me this.'

He passed her the letter and was evidently so angry he could not keep still but marched up and down the great marble-floored drawing-room, looking as if he were quite capable of picking up the furniture and throwing it into the sea.

'Dear Mother,' she read, 'please don't be cross but I'm writing this from Moscow as I know you and my stepfather will be worried that I never arrived as I should have. But quite accidentally I was sitting next to a nice Russian diplomat who said he had known father well and would I like to go to Moscow on my way to Athens to meet some other friends of my father who was very much respected there? Mr Karai said he would fix it up there and then, so I went on from Rome and about six hours later I was standing in Red Square looking at the Kremlin. It's terrific here and I'm being very well looked after by a Russian Colonel who has a large apartment near the Kremlin. I can come on to Athens whenever I like, but I'm enjoying myself so much I'd rather stay on a few days here even though I'll miss the fireworks and all the other things stepfather is laying on for his party. Tell Lucy I'll make up for it by giving her extra tennis lessons and please don't worry – everything's OK – it was a chance I didn't want to miss. After all father *did* decide he preferred Russia to England and from what I've seen already, he was right. Things are much better here and everyone is polite and correct and I've been practising my Russian which, as you know, I'm going to take as one of my A levels. Mr Karai says he will get this letter to you "at the speed of a sputnik" and he might come on with me to

Greece, as he has to look in on the Trade Fair, though he'll miss the opening as I will – but then it's only a sort of Ideal Homes exhibition, isn't it? So I don't think I'm missing much. Please tell my stepfather not to get in a tiz. They all know him here in Moscow and say they respect him very much but does he really have to go to Pekin? The people I'm with don't seem to think very much of the Chinese. They say the Chinese are a great nation but their present leaders are deviationists and not cultured. I'm being taken to the Ballet tonight. As you know the Russian ballet is the best in the world. Love—Mark.'

When she had finished reading the letter, Elissa looked out at the bluish-purple sea and thought about Paul Tarnham. It was extraordinary how things repeated themselves. She had not really understood her first husband – Panayotis was child's play to the psychology of Tarnham – and now she was ceasing to understand her own son. Perhaps, she thought, Eysenck was correct after all and a person's genes were more important than his environment. There was much more of Paul Tarnham in him than of herself. About Lucy she had no doubts. Her daughter would never light out for Moscow because some strange man chatted her up 'accidentally' on an aircraft.

'Well?' said Marides.

'Well what?'

She could be equally aggressive when she chose. There was a lot of the bully in Marides.

'What are you going to do about it?'

'I don't know. And I wish you wouldn't be so aggressive.'

'Why don't you tell him to stay in Moscow if he likes it so much?'

'You really hate him, don't you?' she walked away from him to the terrace, 'I think that's a disgusting way to behave.'

'Troubles and problems. That's all your first husband brought into the world.'

He followed her out on to the terrace where the servants were making final preparations for the party. Marides waved them away.

'You used him,' Elissa said. 'You didn't think like that when it suited your book.'

She had begun to cry in spite of herself, and this made her angry too.

'I think you can manage your rotten little party yourself. I'm going up to my room.'

He put his arm round her shoulders.

'I'm sorry,' he said, 'I didn't mean to hurt your feelings. It's just that I have enough to think about without a worry like this.'

'Damn them!' Elissa said in a low voice, 'damn the bloody Russians and their filthy KGB. Why can't they leave us alone?'

'It's all right, Lissy, I'll get him back for you.'

She got over the crying with a deep sigh.

'I don't know, Pan. Possibly you're right. If that's what he wants to do . . . only I wish they hadn't pressured him in that way. He's only fifteen.'

'I'll get him back,' Marides said, 'I'll tell Voznitsky to have him sent back tomorrow.'

'Suppose they say no?'

'They'll do as I wish,' Marides said with a grim look in his eyes.

It was a perfect setting for a party. Everything had been prepared on a Roman scale of munificence. The house, sited on the top of a low cliff, gave on to a series of terraces which had been arranged downwards to the private beach, leading in turn to the marina. This at times had the look of a private harbour. Marides' large yacht, the *Myrmydia*, lay alongside its own jetty and half a dozen smaller boats belonging to friends furnished the other bays of the marina. The effect was of a lavishly designed set and the concealed lighting, which intensified in power as evening turned into night, added to this theatrical illusion.

Marides was known throughout the eastern Mediterranean for the parties he gave, and tonight *tout Paris* or rather *tout-Athénes* was there. This naturally included a heavy 'Colonels' contingent' as Elissa called them. Now that the regime had been established for several years, Greek security men liked to imagine that they could merge invisibly into any crowd at any party, that foreign propaganda about the regime was nothing but part of an international left-wing plot headed by the British press and that life in Greece was perfectly normal and free.

Elissa knew otherwise. Now as she watched the great house filling up with her husband's friends, associates and enemies, she was able to spot the Colonels' men in their strategic and tactical positions, some with little tape recorders in their pockets, others with the oily smiles which dictators' lackeys acquire when they are not quite sure of their ground.

Although he had not been asked, Mado showed up and was now talking to Elissa. She had never much liked him nor he her, but now tonight she was glad to see him. He gave her a slight sense of security, even though his 007 days were clearly at an end.

'I don't think you'll be missing many ashtrays tonight,' Mado said, looking at a particularly unprepossessing security man standing underneath the big Renoir which dominated the hall.

'You're wrong,' she replied, 'these are the nights when the "souvenirs" go. The big stuff is safe enough and all the valuable smaller things have been put away. Ashtrays and the like are what my husband calls "consumable party trash". What brings you to Greece this time, Mr Mado? Or are you working for my husband again?'

It gave Mado a jolt to hear her talk of Marides as 'my husband' but he did not betray his feelings.

'Oh! the Trade Fair,' he said vaguely, 'I'm temporarily attached to the British Embassy. What's the news on Mark?'

'You know about that?'

'Didn't Miss Eckersley tell you? I missed my plane trying to discover where he'd gone.'

'He's in Moscow,' Elissa said, drawing Mado to one side so that they could not be overheard.

'Hijacked again? Pan must be delighted.'

'Mark says he went there at the invitation of a Mr Karai...'

'Ah! yes,' Mado said, 'that's who it was. I recognised the face but I couldn't put a name to it.'

'Who is he?'

'He's one of the travelling inquisitors. A KGB trouble-shooter – one of the top ones they send in when anything goes wrong in a particular territory.'

'Mark says in his letter that Mr Karai may be coming to Greece.'

'How nice for all of us! Is Mark staying in Moscow?'

'My husband says he'll get him back,' Elissa murmured, 'and no doubt he will. I'm afraid the whole thing worries me sick. Ah! Helen...' she went on in a normal tone of voice to a youngish attractive girl who was passing at that moment, 'I'd like you to meet Mr Mado from the British Embassy. This is a cousin of my husband's who is working with the United Nations.'

'How do you do?' Helen Stanopoulos said. She spoke

English with a reasonable accent but there was no welcome in her look for Mado and the handshake was hard and insensitive. It was obvious to Mado that she also had a haughty dislike of Elissa.

'As a matter of fact Panayotis is my uncle,' she went on, 'not my cousin.'

'My husband has so many relations,' Elissa said, 'it's an achievement I got as near to it as that.'

She favoured the young woman with a chilly look. She was not going to be put in her place by a jumped-up peasant girl from the Pindus mountains.

'Where's your famous Dr Petrov?' she continued, and before Helen could answer, pressed on in a way which made Mado smile, 'Miss Stanopoulos is working on ocean-ography with a world-famous Russian expert. They're quite inseparable.' Then with a side glance at Helen, 'I'm surprised you let him out of your sight at a party like this.'

Helen Stanopoulos looked as if she would relish seeing Elissa carted off to Boubolina Street and given a little of the Colonels' treatment at Police Headquarters.

'Dr Petrov is a busy and important man. I'm only his personal assistant.'

The smouldering look in her dark eyes filled in the rest of the story for Mado. She gave him an impression of far greater sexuality than Andrea Eckersley, who now came up to them accompanied by the winsome Mr Dowdall. Andrea nodded at Mado and Helen Stanopoulos and spoke directly to Elissa.

'Do you think Mr Marides would object if we took some celebrity photographs at this party?'

'I should think he'd hate it,' Elissa said, 'but you could always ask him.'

'Could you do it for me?'

'No,' Elissa said, 'I think it would be better if you approached him yourself.'

'Come with me,' Helen said to Andrea with a snide glance at Elissa, 'I'll ask my uncle in Greek.'

Elissa smiled sardonically at Mado, and when they had moved away, said in a quiet voice: 'You see how it is?'

Mado saw how it was all right.

'Which is the famous Dr Petrov?'

'Talking to my husband.'

'I think I'll join them.'

'Good,' said Elissa, 'I'll take you across.'

He smiled in appreciation. 'I won't ask for any celebrity photographs, you can be sure of that.'

Although well over three hundred people were now at the party, they were dispersed over the various terraces and beaches so that there was no sense of crush and private conversations between two or three people could take place in privacy. Marides did not even know that Mado was in Athens and his face lit up when Elissa brought him across, but whether it was with pleasure or irritation it was impossible to tell. He had told Miss Eckersley and his troublesome niece that he would do something very Greek to both of them if he heard the single click of a single camera shutter, and had sent both of them away with fleas in their ears. Now he turned on Mado.

'Who asked you to this party?' he said in his most aggressive way.

'I thought I'd give you a treat.'

Marides made a sign to his personal servant who was never more than a few feet away from him, and scowled. For a moment or so Mado thought he might well be thrown out.

'Go and fetch a bottle of the Glenlivet whisky,' he said, 'and bring Mr Mado a very large glass.'

Dr Petrov watched the scene in an uncomprehending way. The man whom Mado took to be his KGB keeper edged awkwardly nearer, and found himself at the receiving end of a typical Marides broadside.

'When I want my conversation with Dr Petrov or any other guest recorded by the KGB,' Marides said angrily in Russian, 'I'll ask for somebody competent to listen in. Now you go down to the lower terrace, my friend, and leave us alone.'

The keeper gave his host a nasty grey smile but moved quickly away looking astonished and shocked. Mado, who spoke and understood Russian as well as Marides, laughed out loud.

'I see you haven't changed,' he said in English. By this time he, Dr Petrov and Marides were alone.

'Itsa one sure thing you can rely on,' Marides said, dropping into his Greek-American accent, which only added to Dr Petrov's embarrassment. He was enjoying himself.

'And what is it this time, George? You asking me for a job?'

'When I work for you, Pan, I never get paid.'

'Huh! that's a nerve you got. You never did what you were told.'

'Well, we needn't go into all that now. I'm on the government payroll again. That was part of the deal – remember? – when we liquidated the Tarnham connection.'

Marides stared at him with his enigmatic hooded eyes. No one, not even Mado, could tell what he was thinking and Mado wondered inconsequentially if Marides ever played poker. Certainly this was no time to ask.

'You visiting? or whatsa the job?'

'I'm temporarily attached to the British Embassy. Commercial duties at the Trade Fair.'

'Ah! yes, the Trade Fair, God bless it!' Marides said in his normal brisk accent. He paused very briefly and then turned to Dr Petrov, saying in Russian: 'This is an old friend of mine, Mr George Mado, who is temporarily attached to the British Embassy.'

Dr Petrov made some non-committal noise. As Mado had talked so far only in English, Petrov did not know if he understood Russian. Mado thought it politic to declare his hand.

'Dr Petrov may not have heard of me,' he said in Russian, a remark which caused Marides to splutter quietly into his drink, 'but I have heard of Dr Petrov and the distinguished work he has done and is doing for the benefit of all peace-loving peoples.' It was a long time since Mado had used the good old tarnished jargon but it came, as always, trippingly to the tongue.

'Dr Petrov works on the seabed,' Marides said, a touch caustically. The remark was easy to cap and he had given Mado the sort of opening he could not normally resist. Tonight, however, he managed to control himself.

'That's what I mean,' Mado said in such a way that his sincerity could not possibly be doubted, 'I have heard other great experts declare that the seabed may well hold the key to the future of all of us and Dr Petrov, perhaps, knows more about this subject than anyone else in the world.'

He was beginning to regret bringing the word 'bed' into the conversation, and he saw that Marides was enjoying his discomfiture to the full.

'Of course,' said Marides, 'and that's why Dr Petrov is here tonight. There are more top experts per square inch in Athens at the moment and therefore, naturally, here at my house tonight, than anywhere else in the world.'

'What a pity they can't stay in Athens,' Mado suggested,

43

innocently raising his eyebrows at Marides. 'It would be so good for Greece.'

'I think our friend feels that way,' Marides said in English to Mado. 'The seabed is not the only one he's interested in . . .'

'Very nicely put, if I may say so.'

He saw another man approaching. The keeper had rustled up the big red chief. On a quick look from Marides, Mado bowed slightly to Dr Petrov and said in Russian: 'I sincerely hope we may meet again. I am always available at the British Embassy and perhaps, if you can spare the time, you would do me the honour of lunching with me before going back to Russia.'

'That would be a pleasure,' Dr Petrov said, suddenly grasping his hand, and then as the stranger came into earshot, he went on in a slightly louder voice, 'I am not an expert in the commercial possibilities of the work I do – I leave that to men such as Mr Marides. But perhaps there are Anglo-Soviet links of friendship we can explore under the proper conditions.'

Mado smiled briefly and slipped away. He had not met Voznitsky before but he recognised the Resident from his London briefing. As Mado navigated an oblique route towards the unblended malt whisky, he realised that Voznitsky was only too well aware of his own identity. At this stage Mado had no wish to endanger any possibility that might mature with charges of 'provocation', a standard protective move in the diplomatic game of chess.

'I am sorry to interrupt,' he heard Voznitsky say to Marides as he moved away, 'but there is a French oceanographer I would like Dr Petrov to meet . . .'

He did not hear the Resident add: 'Now that's an interesting face! What a collection of talent you have here tonight *o kyrios* Marides!'

3

Behind the polished exterior and the cold, diplomatic smile, Voznitsky, in fact, was very angry indeed. What was the spy, Mado, doing in Athens? And at a party such as this? It added to the many imponderables of his current life and this inner insecurity, in turn, generated an anger.

What made it worse was that there was no one upon whom he could properly vent this emotion right away. He could scarcely find reason to upbraid Dr Petrov, whom privately he thought a pompous fool, for talking to his host – and coincidentally Mado. Certainly he had at once reduced the junior 'guide and companion' to a state of quivering pulp for allowing himself to be sent away from his sentry post in action. But what could you do with a western millionaire who only played along with the double talk and the protocol when it suited him?

Marides had correctly identified the guide and companion for what he was – a junior officer in the KGB. He had been extremely outspoken and rude. But if a host chooses to be rude at his own party, a guest has only one recourse – to be rude back, if necessary, and to leave. In the case of Voznitsky and the other Russians in the front line at this stinking capitalist party, both actions were out of the question. They had to stay on and suffer.

It was true that Dr Petrov was only under normal precautionary surveillance. He had never at any time in his long and distinguished career given the slightest sign of disloyalty to his country or to the creed of communism, whatever that might happen to be at the time of asking. He did what he was told in everything except his job. In that he was king.

Petrov, so far as was known, manifested a total lack of interest in politics. He had not even bothered to join the Party, despite being invited, since he held himself interested in only one thing – oceanography and its allied subjects – and you did not need to become a member of the communist party to specialise in that.

He had signed no protest letters. He had studiously rejected western propaganda however subtly it had been planted on him. Indeed his record was unblemished and showed that he had always behaved with exemplary sub-missiveness as a senior member of the animal farm. In his own job he was sharp, arrogant, aggressive and, Voznitsky suspected, oversure of himself. Except for Helen Stano-poulos, he behaved as a tyrant to his subordinates who reacted with hatred and fear, but such attitudes were encouraged by the authorities, always provided that an essential loyalty was openly and continuously given to the ideas and practices of soviet communism.

However, there were patent dangers when a knowledge-able man such as Petrov had, for reasons of state, to be sent abroad for international study or work. Inevitably he found himself something of a hothouse flower in these rough western winds. Some hothouse – some flower, Voznitsky thought sardonically. A scientist could not be trusted like a prince of the KGB and now that he was deeply and hope-lessly involved with his personal assistant, Voznitsky sensed that they were all approaching a possible crisis point. The sooner Dr Petrov went back to Russia – or at any rate left his territory – the better for all of them.

When he had steered Petrov into safer hands, Voznitsky

looked around to see what his wife was up to. Decked out in her best outfit, she had had her hair done by the smartest hairdresser in Athens so that she looked like a bourgeois wedding cake, and although she was as disgusted as he was by this western opulence, she seemed to be having little trouble in taking in her fair ration of champagne and smoked salmon. He strolled across.

Irina was talking to that redheaded English woman reporter who had only recently arrived in Athens. So, having nothing else to do for the moment, and telling himself that it is a first principle of war to know your enemy, he contrived as pleasant a smile as possible and decided to ask his wife to make the introductions. As he arrived on the scene, Andrea was saying: 'You Russians put us to shame – you all speak English so well. Where did you learn it?'

'In school, of course,' Irina said gruffly, 'our English schools are excellent.'

In point of fact Irina did not speak English with any fluency and Andrea knew it. It was at once obvious to Voznitsky that she was merely being polite and he wondered what information the girl was trying to prise out of his wife. Certainly the English girl was very attractive. Moreover since he had seen her talking to the spy Mado, no doubt she was a trained security agent as well. He studied her as they talked, wondering if she would be worth pursuing sexually and what else might be got out of it that way. He became uncomfortably aware that his wife was reading his thoughts and decided to move on. He would start a file on Andrea Eckersley in the morning.

Andrea watched him go with amusement. Although this was the first time she had worked for British security, Voznitsky fitted the briefing she had been given by Padstow and, in any case, she had read most of the current output of espionage books so that she knew the scene. It surprised her to see how true to life certain matters of which she had read were proving to be. It gave her a twinge of discomfort and, possibly because she had never done this sort of thing before, she wondered in passing why it was that someone like George Mado had become so cynical about it all. Or was this merely a pose?

Mado came up now a glass of whisky in his hand.

'Hallo, Andrea,' he said, nodding at Mrs Voznitsky who nodded back and immediately moved away, 'I'm sorry you had a bad line on the photography.' And then when the Russian was out of earshot, 'You see the effect I have on our Soviet friends?'

'I shouldn't take it to heart. Or were you going to make a pass at her as well?'

'Not even in line of duty,' Mado said, taking it on the chin. 'Passes at Rooshians add to Confooshians.'

'And the Great Spy is not a Confucian?'

'Oh! God,' Mado said, 'that's the sort of joke I make.'

He took her by the arm and led her out on to the terrace. She was nice and firm to the touch and did not stiffen and resist as he had half expected.

'You're very saucy, aren't you, on your first assignment?'

Now she did suddenly stiffen and turned to look at him in surprise. He dropped her arm and, leaning against the balustrade, studied her anew. Then she relaxed.

'Oh! you mean in Greece? Yes, I suppose I am. But that's all front. I'm dead scared underneath . . . by a man like Marides, I mean.'

Something about her manner did not ring true. She had given herself away and alarm signals were sounding in Mado's mind. Instantly the whisky fumes cleared and he lit a cigarette, watching her keenly through the smoke.

'What other first assignment are you on?'

'Look, Mr Mado, I'm purely and simply a journalist.'

'Pure and simple you may be, but only a journalist – no.'

They looked at each other. She tried to appear puzzled but only succeeded in conveying the sudden fear she felt. The intimate twinge had now turned into a tingle of panic.

'Which of your Maoist friends have you orders to meet in Athens? You don't have to tell me, sweetie, because I shall surely find out, however good your cover story may be.'

He read her like a book but was surprised at the glint of relief which crossed her face. Perhaps Maoism was the wrong tack to take. There were others he could try and he now drew one more bow at a venture.

'That's why you sat next to Mark Tarnham in the aircraft, wasn't it? You were working with Ivan Karai.'

Now she was not being devious at all, but was clearly speaking the truth.

'If I knew anyone called Ivan Karai, I certainly wouldn't be working with him. I simply don't know what you're getting at.'

'No?'

'Honest.'

He believed her. So what could it be? He racked his brains in the pause which followed. It was then that the unlikeliest possibility of all danced up to the forefront of his mind.

'Do you by any chance know anyone called Padstow?' he asked, 'John Padstow?'

She looked stunned and it was lucky they were in a comparatively underlit part of the terrace.

'How did you guess?'

He gazed out across the bay at the moonlight sparkling on the dark Aegean. Soon the fireworks would begin – perhaps in every sense of the word. Then he gave a short humourless laugh.

'The bastard!' he said in a casual voice, 'the cheeky young bastard!'

Then, to her relief, he went on: 'All right, gorgeous, we never had this conversation. OK? You never gave a thing or yourself away and I'm slightly the worse for Mr Marides' excellent Scotch.'

She touched his hand spontaneously. 'Thank you. You're great.'

'And how!' Mado said sarcastically, but letting his hand enclose hers for a moment or so. She was a nice kid for all the up front pretence.

It seemed to Helen Stanopoulos that the whole world was watching her at this party in a hostile way. However intellectually she could rationalise the relationship between Smootchi and herself, however much she could persuade herself that neither of them really cared, that it was simply a passing thing, a private and temporary arrangement – she nevertheless found herself consumed by jealousy and guilt. Jealousy of her Sergei's wife, family and position in Moscow, and guilt because she could not display openly what every girl of her age longs to do.

She was a Greek to her marrow and had an almost bio-logical need to draw attention to the big catch on the end of her line. Her contemporaries were adept at showing off and Helen was no exception. However, not only could she not demand the attention an attractive girl of her age requires, she was forced to creep about at her uncle's party as if she were nothing more than some drab secretary who had achieved a slightly ludicrous position with the United Nations.

Sophisticates would take her as a nonentity, a person of little consequence instead of someone who could proclaim from the housetops that she had been to bed with the greatest oceanographer in the world. It was humiliating and to this had been added the totally unexpected snub she had received from Uncle Pan when she had taken over that impossible woman journalist who had wanted photographs of the party.

She had further alienated Elissa – not that she cared about that – but her *philotimo*, her pride had been hurt. She knew that all Greeks are thought to be fixers at heart, but a fixer has to deliver. She had only asked Uncle Pan this tiny favour on the crazy English woman's behalf, and he had shut her up with a snap. It was intolerable. She felt like crying and the champagne in which she tried to drown these feelings only depressed her the more.

Mado had been watching this almost visible train of thought working in the girl as the party wore on. So picking a moment when she was alone and disconsolate, he took a second bite at the cherry. He came up beside her as she stared unseeing at the firework display.

'A pretty girl like you has no business crying on a night like this.'

'I'm not,' she retorted. 'And anyway it's none of your business. Who are you anyway?'

She looked at him with hot, angry eyes and then answered the question herself: 'Oh! you're the man from the British Embassy my uncle introduced earlier on.'

Everyone else at the party might know who George Mado was, Helen Stanopoulos neither knew nor cared.

'That's right,' Mado said, offering a cigarette and lighting it, 'I shouldn't be upset because your uncle bit your head off just now. He'll have forgotten it all.'

'Oh! I don't care about *that*,' she said, 'my uncle can go screw himself.'

'That's a big statement in dictator land.'

'I'm not interested in politics.'

'I dare say you aren't. Unfortunately Big Brother gets interested in *us*. You're too young and attractive to get hung up like this.'

'How do you know I'm hung up?'

'I don't. But there's obviously something wrong. I'm just trying to help. Really I am. I think you're a smashing girl.'

She glanced at him suspiciously before returning her gaze to the distance, lost in her own perspective.

'Are you making a pass at me?' she asked in a disinterested voice.

'No,' Mado said, 'for once I'm not, though I might get around to it later on. Like I said before, I'm just trying to help.'

For all the occasional vulgarity of approach, Mado was at heart a sympathetic and affectionate man. He had a warm heart and a magnetic hold over women. Although now there were other more sinister motives in his approach to Helen Stanopoulos, they were secondary – as they had been throughout his life – to a sincere urge to help, comfort and restore any woman in genuine distress. Women on whom he concentrated knew and appreciated this warmth. They responded instinctively by trusting him and very often later on by giving themselves to him.

Helen Stanopoulos was no exception to the early part of this process. Under his skilful questioning, which she did not even notice, she began to talk about herself, about her childhood in the Pindus mountains, about the effect on the family which Marides' enormous success had had, about her own brilliance at school so that with minimum help from her uncle, she too had left the village, gone to Athens and had started climbing the scholastic ladder to her present position.

'How many boy-friends did you leave by the wayside?'

'There was only one who really mattered.'

She was obviously caught in her memories and disinclined to go on, so Mado said: 'Why isn't he around any more?'

'Oh! he is. He failed his exams and he's now part of the drug scene . . . and of something else. He thinks I'm unbearably square because I never have been and never will be a dope head. I don't drop and I don't smoke – except straights.'

'You mean ordinary cigarettes?'

'Yes.'

There was a pause as both thought about what she had just been saying.

'But what Nikos really can't stand is ambition. He has no respect for the great things and the great people.'

'And you have?'

'Oh! yes,' she said, a little solemnly like a child, 'that's what brought Sergei and me together.'

Mado glanced over to where Dr Petrov was holding court. A paunchy, middle-aged man with a high opinion of himself – but a great person to her . . . The Russians could prevent Petrov talking to anyone not of their choice, they could not apply the same technique to a Greek girl on Greek soil. But it surprised Mado, nevertheless, that they had left her so much alone. The fact that he and she were now having this conversation would be noted in all the KGB reports the following day. However, the conversation was taking place. He decided to press on to the heart of the matter.

'Does he want to marry you?' he asked.

'I think he might like to. But he already has a wife and family in Moscow.'

'I see.'

It was better not to ask any more detailed questions. She

smiled at him wanly. The vibrations were highly sexual and Mado wondered in passing whether the great Dr Petrov could really handle the passion he sensed in the little Greek girl beside him. He felt sad for them both.

'You know a great deal about Dr Petrov's work, don't you?' Mado said, and then in order not to let her think he was about to question her on the matter, went on quickly: 'I need hardly remind you that when Dr Petrov goes back to Russia, you may be at some personal risk – however unpolitical you may think you are.'

She stared at him silently with her big dark eyes. She held her head very erect in an almost regal posture which showed off her slender neck. Mado thought grimly of all they could do to her pliant young body if they once decided to go to work.

'I don't think my uncle would let them harm me,' she said after a pause.

'I wouldn't rely on it, if I were you. And anyway he's off to Pekin in a couple of days.'

'I still think you're being alarmist.'

He shrugged his shoulders. She had never seen the inside of a Russian prison as he had.

'Well, don't eat any apples if you want to stay in the Garden of Eden.'

'Huh!' she said with a break in her voice so that he suddenly realised she was crying, 'is that where you think I am?'

He put his arm round her shoulders, half expecting to be shaken off but instead she snuggled into the shelter of his bulk. That would be in all the reports tomorrow as well.

'I don't know what I can do but you know where to get me.'

'No . . . oh! yes, you're at the British Embassy, aren't you?'

54

How could she possibly have worked at the United Nations and still be so innocent?

'And the name is Mado. George Mado. Just in case.'

'I'd like to die,' she said in a small voice, 'only I haven't the courage.'

'I shouldn't do that, if I were you. An attractive girl like you . . . oh! no, there must be better things in store.'

'Are there?' she said, the tears streaming down her cheeks, 'not from where I see the scene.'

He had the sudden feeling that the weepy might get out of hand. 'Don't let it go completely,' he said, 'I'm with you, sweetie, but this is no time for a complete breakdown. Where are you going after this?'

'Home. I share a flat in Vassilissis Sophia with two other girls.'

'I have a room in the Grande Bretagne which you can always use if you want.' And then, seeing that she misunderstood, went on: 'It's all right, doll, this is not a backhand way of getting you into bed with me. It's there if you need it. Now, put that hard, snappish look back on your face and circulate some more at this elegant party. You and I have been together long enough.'

She did as he told her, tidied her face and mopped away the tears, 'I'm sorry,' she said coldly, 'it won't happen again.'

'Oh! by the way,' he said as they separated, 'what is Nikos' other name? His surname?'

She gave him a look he could not at the time interpret, 'Nikolaides. Nikos Nikolaides. It's easy to remember.' She stopped dead in suspicion. 'Why?'

'You never know.'

'Leave him alone. He has enough trouble in his life.'

'You still care a little?'

'I hate him. And I hate his friends. But I don't want him hurt.'

'Now there's a fine macrobiotic statement,' Mado said as they moved away from each other, 'I even have friends who don't kill flies any more.'

It was four in the morning before Mado 'crashed out' in his bed at the Grande Bretagne and dawn was breaking just over an hour later when the telephone rang at his bedside.

'Mr Mado?'

'Yes.'

'British Embassy Duty Officer here. The Ambassador would like to see you in the Embassy right away. I'm sending a car to fetch you.'

'Right away!' Mado said sourly, 'that's all I need.'

The Ambassador had not given him a warm welcome when he had first arrived in Greece. Now His Excellency, who had himself been got up in the middle of the night, seemed to be coldly furious.

'I don't know what you were doing at the Marides' party last night, but we've now got a first-class crisis on our hands. Dr Petrov has asked for asylum – and for good measure the Russians have smacked in a charge of "provocation", naming you.'

'I don't think we need pay much attention to that.'

'Don't you, Mr Mado? I wish I could agree. Unfortunately you are not the Ambassador and I am. I knew things would flare up when I first heard you were being sent out here. It's always the same with you people. You're always stirring the pot.'

It was a bureaucratic attitude Mado had had to deal with before. All the Ambassador wanted was peace and quiet – and now patently he was not going to get it. Mado kept his temper and let the insulting words go over his head.

'Presumably the Greeks will grant Dr Petrov his asylum?'

'He hasn't asked the Greeks. He came here – to see you. He's in the military attaché's room.'

'Surely the defection of someone as eminent as Dr Petrov is welcome, isn't it? That's one of the reasons I was sent out here to Greece. Or does it mean too much trouble for the Embassy staff?'

'I find that remark offensive, Mr Mado.'

'Oh! dear me, Ambassador, I'm very sorry indeed.' Mado was as angry as the Ambassador and fully prepared to stand up to any pressure the latter might bring to bear on him. Maybe his pension would again be in jeopardy, but this was as much as he could take at that hour of the morning after all that had developed the previous night. The Ambassador was a small man in every sense of the word and Mado felt like giving him a good thump up the knickers.

'Moreover Dr Petrov has not defected,' the Ambassador continued. 'He has brought nothing with him and he states he is not prepared to reveal any secrets he may happen to know. He does not intend to betray his country in any way. He simply wants not to go back.'

'Bully for the West.'

'Mr Mado,' the Ambassador said curtly, 'I'm afraid your behaviour will have to be the subject of an enquiry. I'm not in the habit of being addressed in this fashion in my own Embassy.'

'You asked me what I was doing at Marides' party. I was doing my job. As for my behaviour, Ambassador, or your opinion of it – I am nominally attached to your staff but I am not in any way subject to your control. And you know it. My brief, about which you were fully informed, is that I can call on you and the Embassy staff for any assistance I need. So let's get ourselves straight. I need and require your help now in this very delicate matter. If I don't get it, you may find your own conduct the subject of enquiry. And if you choose to regard that as blackmail or a threat – that's exactly what it is. I can make life much more difficult for you than you can for me.'

The Ambassador was appalled, his neck a turkey red. There goes the pension again, Mado said to himself, but there was no holding him now.

'Just stop behaving like a Maltese Prime Minister and let me get on with what I was sent here to do. Dr Petrov – and what may follow on – is more important to the West than your job or mine. I'll deal with him now and I shall have an urgent cypher to send as soon as I've seen him.'

He strode out of the room. The military attaché, a regular soldier for whom Mado had a considerable respect, was waiting in the corridor and together they went along to see Dr Petrov.

'I couldn't help hearing . . .' the military attaché began.

'Yes,' Mado cut in, 'but never mind that now. Who else has seen Petrov?'

'Except for the duty officer, only myself.'

'Do you speak Russian?'

'I'm studying it but I haven't yet passed my exam. So I said as little as possible.'

'Good.'

Dr Petrov was in a high state of anxiety. As soon as Mado entered the room, he all but ran across and clasped Mado's right hand with both of his. He was shaking with fear and there was almost no trace of the arrogant, world-famous Russian scientist.

'I see you took me at my word,' Mado said in Russian. 'Sit down, Dr Petrov, and we'll have a talk.'

'I am afraid for Helen.'

58

'Yes,' Mado said briskly, 'you have reason to be. Did she know you were going to defect?'

'I have not defected. I have only asked for asylum.'

'We'll deal with that in a moment. Did she know what you were going to do?'

'No.'

'Then have you got her address here in Athens?'

'Of course.'

'Write it down and say – you use French to each other, don't you? Say in French "Please obey any instructions the bearer of this note may give you" and sign it. Better sign it Smootchi – then she'll know it's authentic.'

Dr Petrov looked at him in amazement.

'You know all that?'

Mado stared at him coldly. The whisky-drinking, easy-going man of the previous night had changed completely and he calculated that this alone was adding to Dr Petrov's confusion. The force of personality facing the great ocean-ographer was considerable.

'Come along, Dr Petrov. We haven't much time. In fact it's probably too late already.'

While Petrov was writing out a shaky message in French, Mado tried to decide on the best course of action to adopt. Should he go himself, or send the military attaché? Or should he risk using Andrea Eckersley? If he or the military attaché with their diplomatic immunity were seen trying to nobble Helen Stanopoulos, there would be further charges of provocation and this would give the Greek security forces any justification they felt they needed to get into the act. From then on the future was unpredictable. He picked up the phone and asked for the Hotel Grande Bretagne.

'Miss Eckersley, please.'

He could hear the phone ringing but there was no reply. Either Andrea was in a deep sleep, which was understand-

59

able, or she was not in her room – which was also under-standable. He put down the phone and turned to the military attaché.

'I think you'd better cope with this as discreetly as you can.'

He took the little note Petrov had written in execrable French and passed it across.

'Bring her here if you can without attracting attention. I'll have a short, sharp session with the brave Doctor.'

Now everything began to happen at once. That same morning Padstow in London had just got into his extremely private eyrie, which could be reached from the Cabinet offices without going out into Whitehall, when he was handed one of the shortest Top Secret and Most Immediate cyphers he had ever received in his life. It simply said 'Help!' and was signed Mado. Within half an hour Padstow was en route to Athens but not before the Foreign Office had caught him with an equally urgent dispatch from H.M. Ambassador in Athens: 'Request immediate recall Mado plus cancellation diplomatic privilege. Necessary withdraw recognition. Report follows.'

'I'll see the Foreign Secretary,' his Chief said, 'but it may already have got out of hand.'

'Yes sir,' Padstow said, visualising Mado's pug-like face, 'I'm very much afraid it has.'

In Athens Voznitsky had not been to bed all night. He and Irina had just returned to the block of flats, known to Western diplomats as the Red Compound, where those Russian diplomats who did not live in the Embassy itself were housed, when he was informed that Dr Petrov had given his guide and companion the slip by the simple expedient of asking him to go back for a briefcase he had left in Marides' house and then driving off in the car himself. A little later the man who watched the British Embassy for them had reported that Dr Petrov had driven up, left the car and gone inside. From then on the die was cast. Voznitsky got his Ambassador to put in an immediate protest of provocation in the accepted form, accusing Mado, and he had then set about the urgent task of securing or in some way of neutralising Helen Stanopoulos. This was not quite as easy as it looked.

Whatever the world thinks of the present regime in Greece, the Colonels' control of the country is absolute. Things work and the life, in outward appearance at least, is stable. As in any dictatorship, such stability depends upon a well-paid network of informers and a hypersensitive fear of the police. From the point of view of the KGB Greece is a very different bowl of bortsch from sloppy old England where anything goes and diplomats are assumed still to be gentlemen, albeit with foreign accents, who abide by the rules – at any rate until the abuses become so flagrant that a wholesale removal job becomes imperative. In Greece anything goes nowhere in this respect. Voznitsky, therefore, found it very difficult to operate in a clandestine way outside the strict bounds of protocol.

Later that morning the Russian Ambassador, accompanied by Voznitsky, called on the Greek Minister for Foreign Affairs who was regrettably indisposed, and they were then seen by a high official who turned out to be none other than Christos Marides, the millionaire's only son by his first wife. Christos, dark, good-looking and vicious, had been noted in KGB files as someone to be very careful about but he was also polite to the point of suavity and both cool and competent.

'I will certainly see that what you have told me, Ambassador, is passed on at once to the appropriate quarters but I must observe that Dr Petrov's secretary does happen to be a Greek subject working in Greece and therefore entirely free to do as she chooses. Greece, I need hardly remind you, is a democracy and the liberty of the subject remains absolute under the law. Whatever arrangements Dr Petrov may or may not have had with his secretary, whatever papers she takes or does not take home with her when she goes back to her flat at night are no concern of the Greek government unless a charge of theft is to be preferred and presumably such a charge, if there are grounds for it, would originate with the United Nations and be dealt with by the police.'

'I consider your attitude unco-operative,' the Ambassador said.

A bland smile spread gently over the Greek's face. He was very much his father's son, Voznitsky thought, and determined there and then that he would have to tackle Marides himself.

'I'm so sorry you feel that way, Ambassador. I am only trying to help.'

'Can you at least inform us of the whereabouts of Miss Stanopoulos?'

'Ah!' said Christos Marides, studying his well-manicured nails, 'now that would be a matter for the Missing Persons Bureau and enquiries can only be made there by a relative...'

From the way he fell silent, the Ambassador and Voznitsky thought he might perhaps have something else to suggest but after a pause nothing further appeared to be forthcoming.

'Very well,' the Ambassador said, getting up. 'I shall report to my government the unfriendly attitude of the Greek authorities in this small matter of co-operation for which we are asking.'

Christos Marides showed them politely to the door and

then on and out into the hall: 'And I shall report to my government the great pleasure it has been to receive your visit this morning and to assist you to the full limit of the regulations. Your Excellency is no doubt aware of the fairly lengthy list of matters in Moscow in which our government has long been seeking assistance. If by chance the list has been mislaid, I will be most pleased to furnish you with a copy. Thank you so much for your call, Ambassador, and you, Colonel Voznitsky . . . I look forward to meeting you again socially as we did last night at my father's party, which I hope you enjoyed.'

With a little smile on his lips, he watched them get into their car and drive off. Then returning to his office, he told his secretary to get his father on the private line.

It would have made no difference had Christos Marides chosen to be more helpful. Helen Stanopoulos had disappeared. At least she had gone from the flat which she shared with two other secretaries in Queen Sophia Street, as the British military attaché had discovered to his dismay.

'I'm so sorry, Major Schofield,' said the shiny, self-appreciative Greek security officer who met him at the door, 'but Miss Stanopoulos is no longer here.'

He spoke excellent English. Since he also knew the British military attaché's name, Schofield took the Greek security presence there to be no accident. The next remark, however, startled him: 'Indeed, we are looking for Miss Stanopoulos ourselves. Did you wish to see her for any official Embassy reason?'

'No,' Schofield said, quickly avoiding that particular trap, 'it was purely private.'

'At seven in the morning, Major? How delightfully eccentric! But then you diplomats with your diplomatic immunity can do as you please, can you not?'

The studied sarcasm was almost too much for Schofield to bear. His work naturally brought him into contact with members of the Greek police and he detested each and every one he met.

'That is right,' he said with equally studied politeness, 'we need answer no questions and we cannot be arrested – even for the crime of visiting a person's flat at seven in the morning.'

With a curt nod, he turned on his heels and walked down the stairs to his car. As he got in, he noticed two other cars waiting nearby filled with thick-looking men in dark glasses, very obviously trying to give the impression that they were there by accident. Those are not your friendly neighbourhood police in their Panda cars, Schofield said to himself, thinking ruefully of the quiet Surrey town in which he lived in England, those are the gentlemen from Boubolina Street, fresh from their midnight tortures. Mentally he spat in their faces as he passed.

4

'Well, where is she then?' Marides snapped down the phone to his son, 'surely your people know?'

'We shall find her, of course,' Christos said at the other end, 'but for the moment she's simply disappeared.'

'Then the longer she stays disappeared, the better for all of us – at any rate until Dr Petrov is out of the way.'

'I'll let you know as soon as we get a line on it.'

Marides put down the phone and glared at Elissa.

'First your son by Tarnham: now this. I shall never get away to Pekin.'

'I suppose it's my fault in some extraordinary way,' Elissa said, pouring oil on the flames. 'Anyway she's always been exceptionally rude to me, that girl. So far as I am concerned, she can stay away.'

'Her father would wring her neck and now, maybe, I'll do it for him. This is where I need Mournier.'

He began walking up and down in a rage. Mournier had been his lieutenant but had met a violent end when the Tarnham connection had been liquidated.

'Thank God you haven't got Mournier. Or do you enjoy having people shot?'

'It's always better to shoot first,' Marides said, and meant it. It appalled Elissa that she had married someone who looked on the taking of life as casually as that. But whenever she had had it out with him, Marides had always observed that she would never understand the Greeks. On that basis she did not care if she did.

 T.R.—C

'What are you doing about Mark? Or shall I go to the British Embassy after all?'

'I told Voznitsky last night. He said it would be arranged.'

'Perhaps they'll expect something from you – over Petrov and Helen.'

'What can I give them? Helen's disappeared and Petrov's at the British Embassy.'

'Is that why Mado was here?'

'It wouldn't surprise me. Or they may be after a bigger fish.'

'Who?'

'You'll have to work that one out for yourself,' Marides said, 'last time it was you and me.'

She stared thoughtfully at the hard little man she had married, the embodiment of the tough compact fighter who never gave up and yet who had surprised her so often with his innate tenderness and a sudden capacity for gentleness. He was not what the English call a 'nice' man, but he had once told her with an understanding smile that she was civilising him.

'But I'll put your money in trust,' he added, 'before the process goes too far. Otherwise you might find yourself a pauper.'

He was unique and she was constantly astonished at how much she enjoyed him.

'Don't involve yourself too deeply,' she said, 'I've had enough violence in my life.'

He looked at her incredulously.

'You ask me to get your son back from the Russians. You think they do things for love? Chivalry – that's out in 1917. Gentleness they never had. Huh!' he snorted contemptuously, 'you English! The Russians understand only two things – intrigue and force. You think you can do business with them on any other basis?'

'All right, Pan, spare me the lecture. I don't want you in danger, that's all.'

'You English!' he said, but there was a twinkle in his eye, 'you want the sun to rise in the west.'

'It does,' Elissa said.

Padstow and one of his top interrogators reached Athens in the afternoon and went straight to the Embassy.

'The Russians have demanded access,' Mado said, when the interrogator and Schofield had gone off together to see Petrov.

'Well, that's standard practice.'

'And the great oceanographer says he doesn't intend to talk.'

'Perhaps he will when he settles down.'

'And he wants his Helen.'

'Well, it doesn't look as though he's going to get her.'

Padstow considered the situation for a moment or so.

'What's the next move?'

'I've asked for a frigate from Cyprus – by invitation of the Greeks, of course, on ordinary NATO business. Just in case we have to get him out of Greece in a hurry. I've no idea how long the Greeks will play ball. At present they're turning a blind eye, or we should have heard all about it by now. I imagine it suits them to string it along in that way whilst the Trade Fair is on. But you never know with the Greeks, especially if the CIA gets into the act. Also once the Press latch on to it, anything can happen. By the way, George, the Ambassador wants you removed. You've got a hornet's nest buzzing round your head in Whitehall. How did you manage so much in so short a time?'

Mado told him what had happened.

'You'd better try an apology,' Padstow said, 'and I'll tell His Excellency you'll be disciplined when you get back to England.'

'I'll complain to the Union,' Mado said, but did as Padstow suggested so that the position was 'technically' adjusted.

'I'd like to recommend that Ambassador for another posting,' Mado commented when it was over, 'somewhere down in the Antarctic would do – don't we have an Embassy near Cape Horn?'

Padstow smiled but there was no stopping George Mado once he had started.

'Now I have one for you, Mr Padstow,' he went on, 'what's all this about Andrea Eckersley? Why didn't you let me in on that?'

Padstow laughed. 'I wanted to see how long it would take you to find out. I see the arthritis hasn't set in.'

'Great! Any other little test you'd like me to pass? Perhaps in return you can tell me if she's on some other assignment I don't know about.'

'Why?'

'Because your glamorous Miss Eckersley also seems to have disappeared. The Grande Bretagne say she never came back last night.'

Padstow thought about it for a moment or two, but gave nothing away. He did not seem to Mado to be unduly disturbed.

'With that coloured hair,' he said, 'I don't think she'll be lost for long. Helen Stanopoulos is a much more serious problem.'

Mado wondered what he was holding back. Perhaps nothing at all. But still . . .

'Man, like it looks you don't trust good old reliable Mado in the way you once did.'

68

'No, George, it isn't that. Only until things clarify a little, Rule No. 1 applies and the less you know of the whole the better.'

'Thanks,' Mado said grimly, 'you mean they might nobble me in spite of what I think you called "my protective notoriety" in London?'

But Padstow turned the subject: 'I think you ought to take a trip out to Vouliagmeni and see how the Marides household is bearing up.'

Almost as soon as he left the Embassy, Mado knew he was being trailed. A small nondescript Volkswagen started up with a man and a girl in it and kept two cars behind the hired Simca Mado drove himself. He had been at the game so long, he could have shaken off his watchers without any difficulty at all but now he was curious.

He therefore drove as if he had noticed nothing out of the ordinary and made his way to Constitution Square, parked the car and then walked into the Grande Bretagne Hotel without looking back. Once inside the hotel he collected the key of his room and discovered that the man had followed him in but showed no signs of continuing on to the lift with him.

He checked Andrea Eckersley's room, still with negative results. But she was Padstow's headache now – and good luck with it, he thought. He had expected to be followed to his room or at least to receive a phone call. But nothing happened. He presumed his watcher was still down below and although he could easily have got out of the hotel by the service staircase, he decided to discover what it was all about and went down again to the hall, pausing until he was quite sure he had been seen and then continuing on into the bar. The man followed and when Mado ordered a Scotch, came up beside him and said to the barman in Greek, 'Make it two doubles.'

'All right,' Mado said, 'who are you and what's it all about?'

'Don't you remember last night?' the man said in passable English.

'I don't think we've met. I have a fairly clear idea of everyone I talked to at the party. I don't recall talking to you.'

'In spite of all that Glenlivet you drank?'

The hard cynical look came back into Mado's face.

'No more guessing games, sport. I have a busy day. What's your thing?'

'Let's say I'm one of the staff at Vouliagmeni, Mr Mado. I want to offer you a deal.'

The man's vague familiarity came into clear focus when Mado visualised him in a white waiter's jacket and black bow tie. This one could have been one of the many who had replenished his glass from time to time through that long, long evening.

'Okay,' Mado said, 'that's what I'm here for. To make friends and influence people.'

'We are holding Helen Stanopoulos and we think you might be interested in having her back.'

'Who's we?'

'The people I work with.'

'Obviously, but who are you?'

'Let's say we're just another band of urban guerillas.

'You're very strong on the "Let's say" bit. Let's say who exactly you are.'

But the man only shook his head and smiled.

'Very well. Whose side are you on?'

'Our own.'

'Fair enough. Ask a silly question . . . okay, so what's the proposition?'

'We'll trade you Helen Stanopoulos for six of our men in prison.'

'Here in Greece?'

'Here in Greece.'

'You evidently know a lot about me,' Mado said, 'so you must be aware that I haven't a hope in hell of honouring such an agreement even if I made it.'

'You'll honour it, Mr Mado, because as a precautionary measure our London friends will take your wife Anna and your child into "protective custody". Do you get my point?'

Mado had to admire the skill with which this approach had been made. Anna's instinct had been right. He should never have come to Greece.

'I have no powers of persuasion over the regime here,' Mado said, 'and you know it. You're asking me the impossible.'

'Nothing is impossible if you decide to try.'

'And what if I fail?'

'Then you may never see your wife and child again.'

It was incredible – totally incredible – and yet on this early evening of a hot summer's day in Athens, Mado had no option but to believe it. The bar was beginning to fill up. It would not be too difficult to escape. Mado considered simply walking away from the man and out into Constitution Square. Then he glanced at him again. The man was smiling in the sly, knowing way of the city Greek. His right hand was in his pocket which bulged in an all too familiar way. The man saw that he understood and shook his head.

'You were thinking of walking out or perhaps of suggesting we go to the nearest police station, Mr Mado? You would never make it with a hole through your genitals.'

'Hm!' Mado said, 'I think we'd better have another drink.'

'Endax,' the man said, 'but don't try any tricks, will you? I have something else to show you as well.'

With the speed of a conjuror, he produced from his breast pocket with his other hand, the sinister-looking identity card of the Greek state security police. It seemed to be game and set.

'Of course you'll have to make up your own mind, Mr Mado, on how much of this is true and how much is false. I may really be an officer in the Greek police or I may have stolen or forged the card. I may be one of Mr Marides' staff or perhaps I was simply hired for the night in view of the size of the party. There are a lot of things you will have to take on trust.'

'You wouldn't shoot a man with diplomatic immunity in a public bar in the centre of Athens.'

'How do you know? You're not in England now. I don't think you'll risk it, Mr Mado. You'd find out too late. The gun I have in my pocket is a very quiet one. Suitable for hijackers in aircraft, low velocity – get the point? All I need to do is knock over this jug and glasses on the bar as a diversion, and no one will hear the shot. As you know, a bullet in the crutch would be very painful and could possibly be fatal. There is no diplomatic immunity which would protect you against that.'

'All right,' Mado said, 'you needn't labour the point. But how do I know you've got Helen Stanopoulos?'

'What ring was she wearing last night?'

'A silver one shaped like a serpent.'

The man put away his identity card and produced the ring from his left pocket.

'And in case you don't believe me about your wife and child in London, perhaps this will convince you.'

Away went the ring and out of his breast pocket came a slim diary which he flicked open with one hand, his right hand all the time kept steady on what Mado presumed to be the gun.

'You live at 54 Carnegie Street, SW19, and your wife buys her groceries at . . .'

'All right, all right,' Mado said, 'what do you want me to do?'

'There is only one person who can ask the authorities to release the people we want and that is Mr Panayotis Marides. You will put it to him. Here is the list.'

Once again his free left hand went into his pocket and produced a typewritten list of six names which he handed to Mado.

'He'd laugh in my face.'

'Helen Stanopoulos is his niece. In Greece family connections are very important indeed.'

'All right,' Mado said, 'I was on my way to see him anyway.'

'Don't try and warn your wife in London. It will only make things happen which you might not like.'

'Do I have your word that she and the child will not be touched if I pull off this thing?'

For the first time the man looked surprised.

'You'd value my word of honour?'

'I haven't much option, have I? But in point of fact, yes.'

'You have my word of honour, Mr Mado.'

Mado finished his drink and prepared to pay but his companion made a sign to the barman and no bill was forthcoming.

'A name might help – and where you want to meet me again.'

'Don't worry about that. We'll keep in touch with you. The name is Nikos.'

'Nikolaides?'

The man raised his eyebrows and paused for a moment before answering, 'So Helen told you all that too?'

Mado nodded. 'You're not quite the man I expected.'

'I don't think Helen is quite the girl you think she is. But then she's a Marides.'

'Did she know you were there last night?'

Mado worked back in his mind to the scene on the terrace when she had filled him in about her life. He realised she was more devious than her innocence suggested, but she had spun him that yarn about the boy-friend who had fallen by the wayside, the drug scene bit, the 'I don't want him hurt' cry from the heart – and if all the time Nikos Nikolaides had been to her knowledge but a few feet away, then she must also be a very good actress, and he would have to think it out all over again.

So he was relieved when Nikolaides said: 'No, she did not know I was there. She didn't expect me to be there and I kept out of her way. In a house that size and with the number of people at that party, it was not too difficult a task.'

'You simply picked her up on the way home?'

'Endax,' Nikolaides said, 'and she was very surprised and distressed. However, we are looking after her well. She will survive.'

'Did you also pick up Miss Andrea Eckersley – the red-haired English journalist?'

But Nikos Nikolaides merely smiled: 'I think you had better be on your way, Mr Mado. Panayotis Marides is still trying to get off to Pekin.'

Mado was not the only man to try for a private talk with Marides that day. Voznitsky, too, wanted urgently to see his host of the night before and when he was unable to fix

74

up an appointment on the telephone, decided to go out to Vouliagmeni himself. He had good reason for this. Dr Petrov's defection could cost him his career. Without warning he had been plunged into the most serious and urgent crisis of his life. Others might harbour illusions about the consequences of a defection. Voznitsky had none. He and he alone would be blamed.

He had had no sleep. The Embassy seemed to him like an antheap on which boiling water had just been poured and not the least of his problems would be to disguise as best he could the utter panic he felt. Moreover he was not at all sure of the help he could ask of Marides nor of what he would receive. His excuse for the meeting, however, was that he had heard from Moscow that Mark Tarnham was on his way to Athens accompanied by Ivan Karai. Voznitsky knew what that would mean. Karai would have full investigational powers, every single person and every file in the Embassy would be sifted from top to bottom and he, Voznitsky, would shortly afterwards be heading back to Russia in disgrace.

Yet there was still a chance. Conceivably the British might yield up their unexpected visitor, provided the Greek authorities would bring some pressure to bear. If only access to Petrov could be obtained, Voznitsky felt reasonably sure he could talk him into returning to the fold under promise of a free pardon and no reprisals.

Voznitsky knew only too well the real value of such promises but this would not prevent him offering Petrov the Kremlin itself on a freehold basis provided only that he would agree to come back. The other and equally urgent task was to find and neutralise Helen Stanopoulos. That girl, he suspected, had experience almost as extensive and valuable to the enemy as Dr Petrov himself. In any case it would be necessary to interrogate her and to find out the extent of her knowledge before Voznitsky could have any hope of clearing his own yard-arm.

Voznitsky was not a happy man. Dedicated and indoctrinated as he had been since boyhood, he had now had enough experience of life in capitalist countries to make comparisons. He had also acquired a taste for some of the goodies which the Western way of life provided. This extended well beyond purely material things. In an appalling moment of self-analysis, Voznitsky had realised that the quality of person he had come to know and like was altogether superior in the enemy world.

He was a lonely man. Well, he told himself, there were a lot of lonely men in Russia, who felt as he did, not a few of them in labour camps. Perhaps this very private sense of longing could be explained away as a lingering end product of his aristocratic forbears about which only he now knew.

Whatever the reason – and the exact cause had no importance – Voznitsky had discovered that there were people in the West who, in their own snobbish-decadent phrase, 'talked the same language'. He had met men and women who understood. Friendship had been offered in a way it would never have been in Russia and Voznitsky had once been crying drunk for three days after facing the inescapable fact that to accept such freely given friendship and understanding was – or would very soon be – the end of his belief in communism and the Russian way of life. Once that step was taken there could be no going back.

Irina did not share the same instincts and ideas. She was not a bad person – even allowing for the spiritually destructive work which the KGB forced her to do – but she thought, felt and lived as if this were the only life she had ever or would ever experience and that the only valid truths were those which were self-evidently physical or could be scientifically proved in a material-mental sense. So far as he could tell, she was totally undisturbed by things of the spirit. She had been taught that God was a bourgeois invention and had been used throughout the ages to keep the toiling masses in slavery – or at best to palliate their dreadful living conditions.

Nothing in her experience had persuaded her otherwise. The world was as you saw it, and there was nothing else. When younger she had had a certain animal kindness and she had proved herself a good and loving mother. He was fond of her and he shared her genuine distress at being forced to leave their beloved Boris behind in Moscow. She had a heart.

But heart or no heart, survival was what mattered in Russia. He had no illusions about what she would do if he were to fall from grace. She would cut herself free. She would save herself and Boris, if need be, by denouncing 'her Alexei'. He did not blame her for this. That is how it was and he would do exactly the same. Or would he? As he drove out to the Marides estate, a foretaste of self-sacrifice seemed to present itself for consideration. But he put this quickly away from his thoughts. The fall was not yet certain. Indeed it might never happen at all.

Marides was not available when he arrived but Elissa had him shown in. He did not know whether to take this as accidental or intentional. Marides might well have been there and merely have had other things to do, or be watching them from another room. Elissa received him in the great drawing-room of the house where she had been writing letters at the sort of escritoire which would have been in a museum in Russia. There was an air of royalty in the room which Voznitsky distrusted and yet found fascinating. How was this impression achieved? Where was the palpable fear you felt in the socialist countries? No Russian woman that he knew could look so cool and distinguished, not only blending into but enhancing the background against which she had been set.

'I'm afraid my husband is in Crete, Mr Voznitsky.'

This was a blow and despite his training, Alexei could not prevent a trace of it showing.

'When will he be back?'

'This evening, I hope. Perhaps I can help you instead?'

There was no warmth in her voice. He could not tell if she knew his real job or was merely greeting him as the assistant commercial attaché she had previously met. In any case her dislike was apparent. She looked magnificent, he thought, for a woman of forty. She had the good bones and the breeding of an aristocrat. The firm mouth, the tawny hair – not as red as that girl reporter's – but a sort of clear chestnut, the fine level teeth, the freckled skin and the grey-green eyes – no wonder Marides had undergone all that he had done to get her as his wife, whilst the Tarnham connection was being resolved. Alexei had met her first husband, the late Paul Tarnham, a couple of times. Now that he looked at Elissa, he could not understand how Tarnham could possibly have abandoned such a woman – even for the greater glory of communism.

'Please,' he faltered, 'it's very difficult. I do not really know.'

This was true. He did not know – and had no means of finding out what he needed to know.

'Why don't you sit down, Mr Voznitsky? Would you care for a drink?'

'I think I drank quite enough in your house last night. I hope you received the flowers this morning. It was a wonderful party.'

'Thank you,' Elissa said, 'that was very polite of you.'

In point of fact she had no idea whether he or anyone else had sent flowers that day. Nor did she give it a thought.

The social secretary took care of that. This was just as well since, in the hurly-burly of Petrov's defection, the Ambassador had forgotten to order the flowers and Voznitsky had had other things to do so had not checked up. He found her cold inspection of himself embarrassing and this grew worse when she played one of his own trump cards so that the hand he was hoping to use became even further weakened.

'When is my son arriving in Athens, Mr Voznitsky? And why was he abducted to Moscow?'

This was a tricky question. It was a matter Alexei had intended to dodge but it had been sprung on him before he was ready.

'He should be here by midday tomorrow. I'm afraid I don't know what you mean by "abducted". Your son was invited to spend a few days in Moscow as an honoured guest and as a tribute to his late father.'

The picture he had formed of the great lady received a partial obliteration in what she said next. It also made an appropriate answer extremely difficult.

'Don't give me that shit, Mr Voznitsky,' Elissa said, every word steeped in acid, 'I know perfectly well what happened, and so do you.'

She paused and stared him straight in the eyes, 'Why?'

He glared back at her, trying as hard as he could to find the right thing to say. But the humanity in both of them got in the way. Moreover there was a trace of irony in her eyes which suggested that it did not matter very much what he said – the facts would remain as they were.

'I can't tell you,' he said.

'You mean you can't make it up quickly enough.'

'If you like.'

'Well, thank God, you're human at least.'

And then Alexei Voznitsky, Colonel First Grade in the

KGB Order of Lenin, Star of This, That and the Other, Chief Gauleiter of the Russian sphere of influence in Greece, said something he would never have believed possible, something of which he would have been incapable until the present disastrous situation had broken over his head.

'I don't know what to do,' he said with a grim set to his mouth, 'I'm lost – lost in the great forest.'

'Good heavens!' Elissa said and rang the bell, 'pull yourself together, Colonel.' And then when a servant answered the bell, 'Bring two large Scotch on the rocks.'

When the servant had gone, Elissa said: 'In all my experience of dealing with you people, I've never had such a statement made to me – never once. What were you hoping my husband would do for you?'

'I need to see Dr Petrov. He has lost his head.'

'And you're intelligent enough to know you're going to lose yours.'

'It's possible. It's not likely – but possible. It is scarcely my fault.'

'That's the last thing that matters. You'll be blamed.'

'Not if I can get him back.'

He found himself being studied attentively again by those cool, questioning eyes.

'How can you make yourself do such a job?' she asked, 'a sensitive, intelligent man like yourself?'

He managed to achieve a tiny smile. He was a strong, good-looking, powerful man with unwavering eyes, who had trained himself to act as if everything he said was sincere. He was a past master in the ultimate swindle but the fact that he knew this in his being made his next remark all but grotesque.

'It's my karma,' he said.

She laughed outright but there was very little jollity in it.

'Then there's no hope at all. A Colonel in the KGB who thinks he has karma . . .'

The drinks were brought in, together with a slip of paper for Elissa. She looked at this and then said to the servant: 'Ask him to wait.'

When the servant had gone, Voznitsky said: 'If you reveal anything of what I've just said, I'll deny every word.'

'And who do you think will care? Why throw yourself on my mercy in this crude and clumsy way? You can't honestly imagine I'm going to help? I've seen what it's like in your communist paradise. I know. Surely by now your people must have appreciated that I'm not and never have been on your side? I loathe and detest what you do and everything you stand for.'

'That is not our information,' Voznitsky said with a stony face. Then, after a pause: 'But, please, I was only talking to you as one human being to another.'

'You do presume, Colonel, don't you?' She mimicked him, 'One human being to another indeed! What sort of treatment would you be handing out if our roles were reversed? You know the answer very well indeed. There would be no mercy from you. Then why presume on me? When have *you* ever helped anyone in *your* life?'

'That is only known to myself and God.'

'Then God help you now,' Elissa said curtly and rang the bell, 'because I doubt very much if anyone else is going to.'

He thought she was asking him to leave when the servant appeared but instead a further shock was in store.

'Ask Mr Mado to come in now,' Elissa said, and then when the servant had gone, 'you may well stiffen up, Colonel, Mr Mado knows what the inside of the Lubyanka is like; he may be able to give you a wrinkle or two on the way to behave.'

'I do not wish to meet the spy Mado.'

'Then you are at liberty to go,' Elissa said, getting to her feet. 'You asked yourself here. You have only to go through that door. I will tell my husband of your visit and if you will write down what you would like him to do, I will see that he considers your request. In the meantime I await the safe arrival of my son, Mark, for which we hold you totally responsible as the senior KGB officer here in Greece. And I warn you, Colonel – should Mark's arrival be delayed, my husband will make things even hotter for you than they are at present. He has a certain power with your people, as I think you know. He won't hesitate to use it.'

The door opened and George Mado was ushered in.

5

Mado paused for a second or two as the door closed behind him. With his mind full of what had just happened at the Grande Bretagne, worried about Anna and the child and trying to contrive how he could best get Marides to do as he wanted, he had certainly not expected to find Voznitsky there. He glanced first at Elissa and then at the Russian. He needed to work very fast indeed and for a moment or so could think of nothing to say. Then Elissa came to his rescue.

'I don't know if you met Mr Voznitsky last night, Mr Mado?'

She waved a vague introduction with her right hand.

'How do you do, Colonel?' Mado said, seizing the initiative. 'No, we didn't meet last night. We simply admired each other from a distance.'

Neither he nor Voznitsky offered to shake hands. Voznitsky conceded him the briefest of nods, at which Mado smiled. Now that Mado had taken the advantage of speaking first, he pressed on ahead.

'Although I have the impression – I can't think why – that the Colonel doesn't think very highly of me. Odd, isn't it? The more so since I have a high regard for him.'

'Are you trying to provoke me, Mr Mado?'

'Here we go again,' Mado said with a contemptuous smile. 'Provocation! It's a great word. You know . . .' he switched to Elissa, 'there are some days when you can't remark on the sun shining in the sky without a charge of provocation from the Russian Embassy. No, Colonel, why should I bother to provoke you? You have enough troubles of your own and no doubt that's why you're here.' He turned again to Elissa, 'I gather Pan is in Crete?'

'Yes,' Elissa said, 'but I expect him back at any moment. As you know, he's trying to get away to Pekin.'

'Please,' said Voznitsky, 'I think I will return when Mr Marides has come back.'

'Why not wait a little longer, Colonel,' Elissa said with an imperious undertone in the voice, 'now that I've brought you and Mr Mado together, I'm sure you have mutual interests you might care to discuss.'

'I don't think so,' Voznitsky said. He appeared to be very cold and correct, but from Mado's previous experience of the KGB and the terror structure on which it is run, he had no doubt the Russian was in a fine old tiz underneath.

'Come, come, Colonel,' Mado said, 'we are on neutral ground. Neither Mrs Tarnham – I beg your pardon, Mrs Marides, nor I are trying to trap you in any way.'

He looked Voznitsky straight in the eyes: 'I won't say we could ever be friends. However, there might be the possibility of a deal.'

'You have great impudence, Mr Mado.'

'We have Dr Petrov.'

'I don't know what you're talking about.'

This was too much even for Elissa: 'Don't be ridiculous, Colonel. Or I shall talk about karma. Mr Mado is being strictly accurate when he says there may be the possibility of a deal.'

'Depending, of course, on what the Colonel has to offer,' Mado put in. All this time the two men studied each other completely unemotionally as if they were poker players assessing the odds.

'I have no plenipotentiary powers,' Voznitsky said in the

end, 'and I do not mean to be rude,' he went on in a slightly more gentle voice, 'but I do not suppose Mr Mado has either.'

'Correct. But we're talking tactics, not strategy, Colonel. I'm sure we understand each other behind it all – the realities of our respective situations, if you like. Equally I have no doubt that both of us have the power to honour any local arrangements we may agree.'

Voznitsky said nothing. He had never been in a comparable situation before. Moreover he was finding it difficult to maintain his apparent contempt for the spy, Mado. To his private embarrassment he liked the man and was forced to respect his nerve. There were no such characters in the circles in which Voznitsky had passed his life. This in its tiny way merely added to his inner distress, and he cautioned himself to be doubly careful not to show any trace of such feelings to either of the other two.

'You say you have Dr Petrov, Mr Mado, but for how long? We are in Greece, not London, England. We are both visitors in a foreign country. It is the Greek state security police that matter here in Athens. Or am I teaching my grandmother to suck eggs?'

'Your grammar is excellent,' Mado said, 'and mine's dead.'

'Pardon?'

'Not at all. I beg yours.'

Then, seeing that the Russian did not fully understand, he went on: 'Sorry – just a poor schoolboy joke. Yes, Colonel, we do know about the Greek Gestapo. We don't woo it to the extent which you and the CIA do with your immense resources, but we are equally aware of its power. And we are not entirely without friends where it matters.'

This was getting them nowhere. Voznitsky paused for a moment or so and then decided on taking a risk.

'You say you have Dr Petrov. Can you then arrange access?'

'Ah!' said Mado, 'the light is beginning to dawn. Well, now, Colonel, you know how the English behave over these things. If someone asks us for political asylum, we invariably grant it to begin with so that the man in question is in protective custody until the facts are known. Protective of the person concerned – and also to see that our good offices are not abused. After all you may be sending us the great doctor as an agent for yourselves. He may not be defecting at all – you may simply be planting him in our midst. We usually have no objection to "access", as well you know, but we leave it to the character concerned. If Dr Petrov agrees to see you, I've no doubt it can be arranged. Now – what can you offer in return?'

'What do you want?'

'Ah!' said Mado, smiling with his mouth but not his eyes, 'this is getting to be like the fairy-tale about the three wishes.'

Mado lapsed into silence. Presumably, Voznitsky assumed, he was playing for time. Both men looked steadily at each other without saying a word but as if carrying on some private dialogue. Both were aware that Elissa continued to watch them with a degree of impatience. This increased the pressure which both felt and to which both reacted in their different ways. The tension became almost unbearable, but still neither man spoke. Eventually Mado broke the pause, having evidently come to a conclusion which Voznitsky assumed centred upon himself.

'I have a notion we understand each other, Colonel Voznitsky,' Mado said in a calm, deliberate voice. 'We are both men of experience and I imagine you would agree that sometimes it is wiser not to put things into words.'

Voznitsky remained rock still. The implication was

86

obvious. It was himself they were after. It almost took his breath away and his first instinct was to lash out in anger. But the intense training he had undergone over the years now stood him in good stead. He did not indicate by so much as a flicker of an eyelid that he understood what Mado was saying.

'In other words, Mr Mado, you wish to take what Americans call "a rain check" on your own demand?'

'You could put it that way.'

Voznitsky shrugged his shoulders and turned away: 'If that is what you want.'

'Shall we shake hands on that?' Mado said quietly.

'On what, Mr Mado?'

'On our understanding of each other, shall we say?'

Again Voznitsky shrugged his shoulders: 'I do not know what you are trying to commit me to – but if that is all you intend . . . very well.'

The two men shook hands in a crisp, military way and at this point Elissa brought the encounter to an end. She had clearly suffered their presence long enough. She moved slightly towards the door, saying to Voznitsky who followed her: 'I'm so sorry you have to go, Colonel. I will get my husband to call you as soon as he returns. In the meantime you will let me know when my son is expected at the airport, won't you?' She turned and stared coolly at him, 'I am sure you and I understand each other too.'

She saw him to the front door of the house. As soon as he stepped outside, his car drove up and after he had gone she walked slowly back to the drawing-room, where Mado had remained by the doors to the terrace staring out at the deep blue sea.

'I'd better go back to the Embassy, too,' he said.

'I think Pan would like to see you first. I'll call him.'

Mado grinned. This was more like the Marides he knew.

'He never went to Crete? He was here all the time?'

She smiled in a cat-like way.

'He returned about ten minutes before Voznitsky arrived. He didn't want to get involved until he had more information at his fingertips.'

'I have some very hot information indeed,' Mado said, thinking back to his meeting with Nikos Nikolaides in the bar of the Grande Bretagne, 'but I also need to get back to the British Embassy fast.'

'All right, Mr Mado, I'll . . .'

'Look, Mrs Marides, stop putting me in my place. You and I have known each other a considerable time. I know you don't particularly like me . . .'

'You're quite wrong there.'

'But surely if Pan calls me George, you could manage a little less formality.'

'I'm sorry, George,' she said, with an unexpectedly warm smile, 'it's all my fault. Perhaps you don't realise how shy I am. You know, if you marry someone like Pan and take on all this . . .' she indicated the house with a wave of the hand, 'jealous relatives, a son by the first wife who would quite gladly see you dead . . . well, you know my background and my circumstances . . .'

'Okay, doll, I'm sorry to dot the i's and cross the t's but I think you may have me in the wrong perspective, too. You think I've only one idea in my head where women are concerned.'

'That's pretty well so, isn't it?'

'It's only part of the truth. Of course I'll lay any attractive bird who shows willing, even if it's only by the flutter of an eyelid – but there are other things as well. I have a young wife and a very new child. They mean as much to me as . . .'

'My family means to me,' Elissa said. 'Yes, George, I

know. I'm sorry we didn't have this out and settled before.'

They smiled at each other.

'You're not such a skinny, stuck-up bitch after all.'

'And you're not just the elderly lecher I used to think you.'

'What's going on?' Marides said, striding into the room, 'you making the pass at my wife, you failed spy, you . . . ?'

Although Mado was a good two inches taller, Marides thundered up like an irate bull, picked up Mado by his lapels and held him in such a way that it was clear he could have thrown him across the room if he chose. He held him like this for a moment or so and then put him down with a short laugh.

'I don't-a trust you with my grandmother of ninety-two.'

'Yes,' Mado said, straightening himself and wondering who would have come off better had there actually been a fight, 'I went through the grandma bit with our Russian friend.'

'What are you going to do with Petrov?'

'I don't know. It's out of my hands.'

'You know where my niece, Helen, is?'

'No, but I know who's got her.'

'Ah!'

Marides stopped dead in his tracks and for a moment or so froze into a complete stillness.

'Who is holding her?' he asked in a low voice.

The almost instant transformation from raging bull into humming dynamo struck Mado as extraordinary even though he had witnessed it many times before. Marides was dangerous when violent, lethal when he was quiet and still.

'I was approached by someone called Nikos Nikolaides.'

'Yach!'

'You know him?'

'Nikos – no. Nikolaides is the code name for the current

urban guerillas. They operate under cover names. Like in Ulster: like the Tupomaros in Uruguay. What do they want?'

'Six of their people released by the Greeks. He told me only you could get it done.'

'Ay! ay! ay!' Marides sighed and for the first time in his life Mado felt a twinge of pity for the millionaire.

'It was coupled with a threat to me.'

'Why you?'

'I suppose they thought you might listen to me.'

'And what was the threat?'

'To Anna and my daughter in London. That's why I must get back to the British Embassy as soon as possible.'

'You take it seriously?' Marides asked, his hooded eyes brooding over the scene like a vulture.

'Wouldn't you? This is a kidnap-hijacking age. It's all too easy in an open society.'

'Yes,' Marides agreed, 'and it's not too difficult here in Greece.'

'This Nikos was one of your waiters last night.'

Marides said nothing, his mind apparently on other things.

'I need Mournier,' he said eventually and then with a sharp look at Mado, 'you'd better take his place.'

'I can't. But thanks for the offer. I'm working for someone else and I have a pension on the end.'

'Yach! pensions . . . you work for me, you don't need a pension.'

'I can see that, Pan. You mean I wouldn't live to enjoy it.'

'No, I do not mean that. I'll look after you and your family.'

'He will, you know,' Elissa put in.

'I'm not a killer like Mournier.'

'I'll find you a man for that.'

'You'll have me in the Lubyanka again.'

'It's an occupational risk. Anyway, I'm finishing with Russia.'

'I don't fancy the Pekin equivalent. Look, Pan, you know I can't opt out of my British commitments in a five-minute conversation.'

'Leave that to me.'

'I was going to work for you before – and you know what happened then.'

Marides made that little backward jerk of the head with a click of the tongue – the negative "$\sigma\chi\iota$' sign – which is peculiarly Greek.

'That Mournier was a jealous man. Afraid for his job. Well – he had reason to be. He wanted to take me over. Me!'

He gave a short contemptuous laugh: 'You don't-a have such ambitions. Only one thing, George Mado, I catch you making a pass at my wife and . . .'

He drew his finger across his throat.

'Oh! we're just good friends,' Mado said, 'as of five minutes ago. She doesn't fancy me.'

'I'll talk to your people in London.'

'I'll think it over.'

'Oh! no you won't. Yes or no now.'

Mado held the pause for as long as he dared. Then with a little shake of the head and a glance at Elissa, he said: 'Not until I'm released from my present commitments.'

Marides' mouth set in a hard firm line.

'You think I'll hold open the offer?'

'If you won't then we're all of us wasting our time.'

To the surprise of both Elissa and Mado, Marides looked across at his wife with raised eyebrows.

'You think I should wait?'

'Wait,' Elissa said as if the outcome had never been in

doubt. Marides turned his baleful look on Mado and nodded.

'You see who takes the decisions around here now? All right, George, you'd better get back to the Embassy. I have a great deal to do.'

'Like putting off your trip to Pekin?'

'Call me in two hours' time,' Marides said, 'and let me have that list of six names you've got in your hand.'

Mado handed over the piece of paper given him in the Grande Bretagne bar. Then with a smile at Elissa, he left.

The news about Dr Petrov broke via a French paper the following morning. The item was brief and to the point. One of the world's most celebrated oceanographers had disappeared from Athens. The Russians had disclaimed any knowledge of Dr Petrov and referred enquirers to the United Nations who at first denied Dr Petrov's existence, then that he had come to Athens at all, then that he had disappeared and finally, as a last resort, referred callers back to the Russian Embassy. The Greek authorities had no comment to make.

In a matter of hours, specialised members of the world press homed in on Athens. Andrea Eckersley's editor in London thought that her presence there might well put the paper ahead of the crowd and waited impatiently for her story to arrive. It was unlike her Little Ladyship – her label when things went wrong – not to come up with something bizarre. When several deadlines had come and gone, however, a phone call to the paper's local man in Athens revealed that Andrea, too, like Dr Petrov had disappeared off the scene. After one or two sharp remarks about the reliability of ladies with red hair, the group's top Kremlinologist hurriedly flew to Athens. But by the time he arrived, other developments behind the scenes had already taken place.

The Royal Naval frigate, which Padstow had requested, had arrived in Piraeus 'on a normal courtesy visit' and a party of officials from the British Embassy, all with diplomatic privilege and all conveyed in official Embassy cars, had visited the ship. Amongst these was someone well shielded from casual eyes but who looked like Dr Petrov. Technically Greek security could have 'cut out' any of this visiting party at the point where they left the Embassy cars at the foot of the gangway leading up to the British warship. At that point anyone without diplomatic immunity was for a few moments on Greek soil and therefore unprotected by the international umbrella.

But when the cortège of cars drove up to the ship, Greek security police proved to be conspicuous by their absence. To all outward appearances the position was simple. A British warship had arrived in the port on a friendly visit and some of the local Embassy staff had gone on board for a drink.

'However, any idea that the Greeks are unaware of what's going on,' Padstow said to the military attaché, when the transfer operation had apparently been successfully completed, 'is pure mythology – and mythology began with the Greeks.'

This, indeed, was true.

'He's thought to be on board HMS *Jasmine*,' Christos Marides said to his father, when he arrived for dinner that night, 'and the Nix have got Andrea Eckersley as well.'

'Who's she?' Marides growled.

'The red-haired journalist who was here the other night,' Elissa put in, 'the one who's going to do your profile for her paper. We had a letter from the editor – remember? And she wanted to take photographs of your party.'

'What's the interest in her?'

Elissa said nothing. The introduction Padstow had provided was entirely private to herself. She might tell Pan about it later on, if by then he had not already guessed. She was certainly giving nothing away in the presence of Christos, who in any case answered the question.

'She probably has an intelligence assignment,' Christos said, 'in addition to her role as a journalist.' He shrugged his shoulders, 'though not a very important one, I imagine. At any rate she's of little interest to us. She has never attacked the regime. She's no Lady Fleming.'

'Then why should the Nikolaides bother?'

'They may want something from the British press.'

'Yach!' Marides said, evidently dismissing it from his mind, 'so how do we get Helen back?'

Now it was Christos who fell silent. He was like his father, Elissa thought, he could drop a mask over himself in a Middle Eastern way which made his thoughts – indeed his whole self – impenetrable to ordinary European eyes. How much did he know? Was he, perhaps, half in with the Nikolaides? He was high up in the Greek Foreign Office – and his father was Panayotis Marides – so naturally his face fitted in with the regime. Or did it? She could not possibly guess.

All she did know for certain was that behind the smiling eyes, the easy glistening charm and the warm, polished manners, lurked an enemy. She did not know why. He would inherit as much of the Marides empire as he could possibly need or want. He was the Crown Prince and she merely the Dowager Queen, to be taken care of later on by a discretionary trust. So it was not – at any rate primarily – to do with money. Why then did she dislike him so much – and feel instinctively that this antagonism was amply reciprocated? Why was she afraid, at times, even to be in the same room?

Marides took out the list of names given him by Mado, and passed it over to his son.

'I know none of these people. Would it hurt *o kyrios* Lamda to set them free?'

O kyrios Lamda – Mr L – was the way Marides referred to a certain Lycopoulos who was currently the man in the regime with the power to make the Minister of Justice and the Head of the Security Police do as he wished. On the basis that all dictatorships are run sooner or later by those who control the secret police and their files, Mr L was, at that time in Greece, the quiet, unknown, rarely seen man with the essence of power in his hands.

Christos shrugged his shoulders: 'I can ask him,' he said. 'I have the number of his private account in Zurich into which you could pay direct. I suppose these people could always be re-arrested unless they went underground straight away.'

'How much would he want?'

Christos made an upward gesture of the eyebrows and clucked his tongue, 'It's more likely to be a percentage of the Pekin deal.'

An expression of acute pain passed over Marides' face. It made Elissa smile and she went over and put an arm round his shoulders, aware as she did so of the distaste she was giving to Christos.

'She's your niece, Pan,' she said ironically, 'and it's only money.'

She thought he was going to explode and for a second or so wondered if she had gone too far. Then unexpectedly he laughed.

'All right, Christos,' Marides said, 'you do the preliminaries and I'll talk to Mr L tomorrow. What do the Nix want for – what's her name? Miss Ackity?'

'I don't know. I'm not directly in touch – obviously. I

doubt I could find that out without prejudice to my own position.'

But Elissa noticed that he was careful to look away as he said this so that his eyes could not be seen.

'Why do you ask?' Christos demanded.

'I'll have her back as well. She's here for one of the Sundays, isn't she?'

Marides waited for a reaction from Christos and Elissa. He had the crafty look of a merchant in the *souk* about to dispose of a dubious jewel.

'My niece's life story could cost a newspaper a sizable sum of money. Of course,' he added, 'it will be worth it in Fleet Street terms – so perhaps everyone will make money in the end.'

6

Within a few hours of Dr Petrov's supposed arrival on board, HMS *Jasmine* was ordered to sail from Piraeus 'for an unknown destination'. A team of highly sophisticated interrogators from British Intelligence had been flown out to Athens and some of these also went on board the warship.

'You'd better get down there as well,' Padstow said to Mado in the British Embassy, 'you're certainly a familiar face to the Greek security forces.'

'Don't you think I'd be more useful here? What about the Nevsky Prospekt – Voznitsky, I mean?'

'Well . . .' Padstow hesitated, 'it's difficult to assess. I'll get you back here just as soon as I can. I don't think that'll come to a head quite as yet.'

'And Helen Stanopoulos?'

'I'll keep in touch with Marides. I've asked London for special protection over the next few days for your Anna and the child. I'll get someone to chat her up so that she'll know what's happening and won't be afraid.'

'She'll be scared all right,' Mado said grimly, 'and angry as well. You tricked me with this assignment, John, you've a lot of responsibility for what's happened.'

'Don't kid yourself,' Padstow said, with an attempt at lightness, 'you're having a whale of a time.'

'Marides wants me to work for him.'

'Why don't you, George?'

He smiled at the pug-faced man who was, in fact, far more valuable to the firm than the establishment was prepared to admit. 'You'd make a lot more money than you would with us.'

'I had a desk job and a pension. Now look what you've done.'

'You were bored to distraction.'

'I'm getting too old for this sort of thing.'

'Nonsense,' Padstow said impatiently, 'you're just entering your prime. Off you go now with your bag of red herrings.'

Mado thought about this for a moment or so.

'What if Petrov still won't talk?'

'You know the answer to that, George, as well as I do. The Russians can have him back. However – with our friend Voznitsky in mind – perhaps not quite yet. The inquisitor is due to arrive tomorrow.' He visualised the scene and laughed, 'Mr Ivan Karai is a very very nasty piece of work. Voznitsky isn't going to have a nice time at all. That should console you when you start to feel seasick on board HMS *Jasmine*.'

'So be it,' Mado said, going to the door, 'at least HM ships still carry duty-free Scotch.'

It was just as well, from Padstow's point of view, that Mado had disappeared temporarily off the scene since a few hours after HMS *Jasmine* had sailed, an ominous message came through from London. Mrs Mado and her child were not at home. A neighbour had seen the milk bottles collecting outside the door and the local police had broken in. There was evidence of a hasty departure and the phone had been knocked off its hook. The Nix, it could only be presumed, had effective associates in London.

At much the same time Marides received a phone call

98

giving him forty-eight hours to secure the release of the six whose names he had already placed in front of Mr L. Otherwise Helen Stanopoulos and Andrea Eckersley would both be executed when the deadline expired. The tension began to build up.

'Your son by Tarnham is supposed to arrive tomorrow morning at midday,' Marides said sourly to Elissa, 'and I've postponed my visit to Pekin.'

'Did you see Mr L?'

'I saw Mr L to the extent of a million Swiss francs. But it's not as easy as that. Mr L has to carry other people with him on this. Accidents can always take place: not least of all to Mr L himself. He's very much aware of the dangers.'

'If you live by intimidation,' Elissa said, looking hard at her husband, 'blackmail becomes an operational risk.'

'What kind of talk is that? Are you addressing a meeting?' Marides said contemptuously. 'All business in this part of the world relies on intimidation and blackmail – at any rate to a certain degree.'

'And you call a million Swiss francs a certain degree?'

'It's recoverable,' Marides said, 'the life of my niece is not – once it's been taken.'

'When is Mr L going to act?'

Marides shrugged his shoulders. Normally when he was in such a mood, Elissa would have left him alone. Now she could not free herself of the anxiety in the air.

'Do you really trust Christos?' she blurted out, realising from the glare she received that this was precisely the sort of question he did not like her to ask.

'What's wrong with you, Lissy? Why suggest a thing like that? Do you trust your own son?'

'My son is fifteen. Yours holds a somewhat different position.'

99

'Yach!' said Marides, 'I trust myself, that's all. And sometimes I have doubts about me.'

Padstow had been right, when commenting to Mado that Voznitsky was not having a nice time at all. Predictably Moscow was furious about the Petrov defection and the silent, internally applied terror began. Karai made it clear, when he arrived, that a full inquisition had been ordered and that he himself had plenary powers. The fact that Karai was junior in rank to Voznitsky and treated him with the polite deference a Resident expects to receive, only made the realities of the situation more deeply sinister in their implications to Voznitsky's experienced mind.

However, he was still as of now the Resident, still the local Czar, whatever the threat. It had taken him several sleepless nights to recover from his meeting with Mado. The realisation of where he stood in the British scale of values, compared even with someone of the calibre of Dr Petrov, was not in itself remarkable. What was disturbing – and this nagged at him like a sore – was the insolent suggestion that he himself might be 'ripe'.

Mado had not put it into words but the message had come through all the same and the shock had stayed with him like an ache in the bones. The other factor which these days never left him for long was the magnetism Elissa exercised on his waking thoughts. It was absurd, it was hopeless, worse – it was fraught with unnecessary danger – but the emotion could not be suppressed. He reflected ruefully that he was like a schoolboy suffering his first experience of romantic love.

She and her daughter Lucy had come to the airport to meet the Roumanian plane from Bucharest on which her son, chaperoned by Karai, arrived at Athens. As Voznitsky watched her getting out of the Marides' Rolls-Royce in the cornflower blue dress which so suited her, and walking so elegantly into the airport, he once again found himself astonished that the defector Tarnham could have abandoned such a woman.

'We kept our promise, you see,' he remarked, as they waited for Mark Tarnham to clear the formalities.

'We should all have been better off if there'd been no promise to keep,' Elissa replied. 'I wish your people would simply leave me and my son alone.'

When Mark came through the barrier almost running, he seemed to be bursting with enthusiasm. Elissa had not seen him so animated since those carefree childhood days before Paul Tarnham had left them and had so ploughed up their lives.

'It was absolutely super,' he said, after kissing his mother and giving his younger sister a perfunctory nod. 'It's been the best trip I've ever had my whole life. This is Mr Karai, Mother.'

'How do you do?' Elissa said formally. She did not offer her hand.

Mr Karai brought his glistening charm to bear and said quickly: 'I hope you've forgiven us, Mrs – Marides. But it has been such a pleasure to show your son something of our great city of Moscow and to make him aware of the esteem in which his father is held by the Russian people.'

Elissa stared at him with an icy contempt which would have withered anyone less armour-plated than a high official of the KGB. Then she turned away and walked towards the car.

'Come along, Mark,' she said, 'you and I are going to have a talk.'

Lucy made a face at her brother whose ebullience drained away like air out of a balloon. Mark shot a furtive look at Karai, from whose face the smile had also begun to fade and at Voznitsky, whom he had not met. He then followed his mother with the despondency of a dog caught romping away on its own.

'Welcome to Greece,' Voznitsky said to Karai, who returned him a cold, ironic smile.

'That remains to be seen, comrade Colonel,' Karai said, 'let us go to the Embassy straightaway.'

The deal by which Helen Stanopoulos and Andrea Eckersley would be set free in return for the release of six of the Nikolaides then in prison, depended – as Marides had forecast – on a number of factors not under the direct control either of Marides or of Lycopoulos. The paramount one was secrecy.

Mr L, though all powerful, had nominally to work through others, since the regime was at pains to play down the dictatorship aspects of the current scene and Marides, on his side, had no wish to encourage further blackmail attempts.

Marides seemed always to be angry these days. He stormed into the British Embassy and demanded a meeting with Padstow, whom he knew to be in Athens. Half the people he asked did not even know of Mr Padstow's existence and when he eventually reached the military attaché, Schofield said: 'He's gone out to Vouliagmeni to see you, sir.'

Schofield was privately appalled at the way a man like Marides could break all the security rules in the Embassy, marching in and demanding to see anyone he chose.

'Yach!' Marides said and turned on his heel.

'Er, excuse me, sir, did you have a pass to get in?'

But Marides had already gone.

'This is going to help us a lot,' he said when he reached home and found Padstow with Elissa. Marides threw down one of the English Sunday papers in which there was an article headed 'In with the Nix' by Andrea Eckersley.

'Have you any idea how that was got through?'

'None whatever.'

Padstow had seen the article before coming out to Vouliagmeni. He, too, was appalled to read how Andrea Eckersley had been 'kidnapped on my way back to Athens after attending one of Panayotis Marides' old Hollywood-style parties'; and how she had then been held incommunicado by the Nikolaides whilst a ransom was negotiated for herself, and the release of important members of the Greek Democratic movement agreed in return for the life of 'the Greek secretary, or Dr Petrov's *petite amie.*'

Andrea had evidently been in communication with Helen Stanopoulos. Indeed from the way the article read, there seemed little doubt that they were held together.

'Our captors tell us in a completely factual way that if a deal is not speedily agreed, we will both be executed. I have no reason to disbelieve this. I therefore asked permission to write what may prove to be my last article for this paper ... the Nikolaides I have met are no ordinary gang of thugs. They are educated, intelligent, middle-class Greeks determined upon restoring democracy to the Colonels' paradise. They are also, so far as I can see, completely ruthless and one hundred percent effective. Helen Stanopoulos and I are merely the trading tokens of the moment and, as one of our jailers sardonically remarked "In Northern Ireland today this would not even get into the papers". There is no doubt we are into an age when human hostages are shopped around like Green Shield stamps.'

This theme was developed in the well-known Andrea Eckersley manner. Unquestionably the article was authentic. Equally certain was the embarrassment it would cause.

'Just another bunch of Palestinians,' Marides growled,

'they want it all ways – the money, the power, the publicity. Take all, give nothing and above all boast. I had it fixed until this. Now we shall have to start all over again.'

For a moment or so nothing was said. All three of them tried individually to assess the possibilities.

'What would be the effect of Dr Petrov's return from limbo? I mean – suppose he decided to have second thoughts?'

Marides stared at him: 'How possible is that?'

'I think the Russians will be given access. He seems disposed to meet them. But I want the offer of this to be handled first by Voznitsky. I'll have Mado back here tomorrow.'

'As a matter of interest – from where?'

Padstow hesitated.

'I shall find out in the end,' Marides went on, 'so you might just as well tell me now.'

'Gibraltar,' Padstow said, 'it's the nearest place unquestionably British.'

'You owe me a thousand drachma,' Marides said to Elissa, 'that's where I said they'd take him.'

'It doesn't sound as if Dr Petrov is being co-operative,' Elissa remarked.

'He's not,' Padstow said. 'All he wants is his Helen.'

'It's proving an expensive taste,' Marides said, 'for everyone else.'

Mado duly returned to Athens, as Padstow had arranged. They met at the airport and together went to the Embassy.

'Fly RAF,' Mado said. 'It's so healthy and quick, but you do miss the pretty hostesses. Now, John, I've one or two bones to pick with you.'

'I know, George, but don't pick them yet.'

'All right,' Mado said grudgingly. 'How's your pretty defector?'

'Obstinate. He's got the full double think going. He won't budge from his original line. He hasn't "defected" – he just wants to stay with his Helen. He's not betraying his country and he's not going to talk.'

'What's the next move?'

'London has reassessed him,' Padstow said, 'and he's come out of it with a somewhat lower rating. Also he's now prepared to discuss his problems with someone from his own Embassy. I want you to offer that one to Voznitsky.'

'How?'

'Marides has agreed the use of his house as before – if that's the way you want to play it – so why don't you get it set up from here and then go on out to Vouliagmeni? Or perhaps you can do it on the phone?'

'You give me the easiest assignments. Who's the next one I nobble? Breshnev?'

'You speak Russian, George, you're the only one who can pull it off with Voznitsky. You're already halfway there. I think he trusts you.'

He paused and looked at him hard: 'I'm desperately sorry I've no good news about Anna but there's a red alert on that one now in London. Everything that can be done is being done.'

'Don't give me that government spokesman stuff. I'd rather go back and find them myself.'

'How? What can you do that isn't already being done?'

'It's my wife and child.'

'I know,' Padstow said, 'I understand.'

'Bully for you,' Mado said. 'That helps a lot. I haven't slept for two nights.'

In fact Padstow had never seen him in such a state.

'You don't catch me this way again,' Mado went on

sourly and picked up the phone. 'Get me the Russian Embassy. I want to speak to the assistant commercial attaché, Mr Voznitsky.'

Whilst Mado was waiting to be put through, Padstow said: 'By the way, Marides thinks that the Petrov scene is taking place in Gibraltar.'

'Who gave him that idea?' Mado said, his hand over the phone.

'I did. It's the nearest place unquestionably British and it's where Marides thought we would take him.'

A glint of a smile came through the tiredness in Mado's eyes. 'What made you pick on the Rock?'

'I've noticed Marides doesn't always know what he lets you think he knows. So I played on his deviousness. Cyprus was too obvious. Malta's too busy being independent – so I settled for Gib; which seems to have been exactly his own train of thought.'

'Well, Master John, you're certainly learning fast.'

'I knew you'd be proud of me, George, even all that time ago in Beirut.'

But Mado gestured him into silence and said in Russian into the phone, 'Good afternoon, Colonel. This is your friendly British spy, George Mado. I suggest we meet where we met before at your very earliest convenience. You won't find it a waste of time.' He put down the phone.

'That wasn't Voznitsky,' he said, 'but it will be interesting to see if he turns up.'

'He'll bring Karai.'

'An added pleasure to look forward to . . . Reach into your bottom drawer, sport, and produce me a Scotch. I suppose we can call on the RAF for some more transport, can't we?'

Padstow nodded: 'You think Voznitsky will trust you to that extent?'

Mado shrugged his shoulders: 'He'll soon be desperate. If he isn't already.' He paused in thought. 'Of course they can always make their own travel arrangements, if that's what they want. It's up to them. What our friend isn't going to pass up, though, is the chance of a confrontation with Dr Petrov. That's the only valid way he has left of clearing his yard-arm.'

They were just leaving for Vouliagmeni when the door opened and the military attaché brought in Andrea Eckersley. She looked distraught and dishevelled, as if she had been sleeping in her clothes, but there was still some sparky fire in the eyes.

'Is this where I get a bath?' she said, flopping into a chair, 'if so, just wheel it in. And I could do with a drink as well.'

Padstow produced another Scotch from his bottom drawer.

'Where did you find her?' he asked the military attaché.

'I didn't. She just turned up.'

'You could put it that way,' Andrea said, 'aren't you going to ask me if I'm all right?' And then, before anyone could speak, 'Well, I am, thank you very much.'

She took a long drink and suddenly began to cry.

'Don't pay any attention,' she said, like a general addressing an army, 'it's the effect of not being shut up in an airless cupboard any more.'

The three men watched her in silence.

'I'd come over and comfort you,' Mado said, 'except you'd misunderstand.'

This made her laugh and she tossed her head in the old defiant way.

'I'm much better than I look,' she said. 'All I need is a dainty dress and I'm ready for the garden party.'

'Who else knows you've escaped?'

She shrugged her shoulders. 'I didn't escape. They took me out in the country last night. They said I'd be shot . . . and I believed them. Instead they dumped me half-way to Delphi. That's why the taxi here cost rather a lot.'

'What about Helen Stanopoulos?'

'I don't know. She's their trump. Me they just wanted to frighten. They succeeded in that.'

She laughed rather shakily but the whisky was taking effect and she seemed to be regaining her composure with every moment that passed.

'You were together?'

She nodded.

'I think they only grabbed me because I saw her picked up so they wanted to shut my mouth.'

'Why did you do that article?'

'I had to. At gun point.'

'Hm!' Mado said, 'something doesn't add up.' He shifted his gaze from Andrea to Padstow, who raised his eyebrows slightly and said nothing.

'What's upsetting you?' Andrea said with a guarded look. She was suddenly made aware of a hard, professional inspection, tinged with possible hostility, which the three men were beaming towards her.

'It's all a little too pat,' Mado said. 'You happen to see Helen Stanopoulos picked up in the middle of the night after the Marides party, you happen to be picked up your-self, you do a highly questionable article for a world-famous Sunday newspaper . . .'

'For which I work.'

'And which blows into smithereens any secret negotia-tions then in progress.'

Andrea sat up, put down her glass and said angrily: 'Are

you accusing me, George Mado? If so, of what? What *is* this – an interrogation?'

'All George said was that it struck him as a little too plausible,' Padstow remarked in what Mado knew to be a deceptively relaxed way. Mado had a long-standing prejudice against upper-class public schoolboys and the way they carried on, but there were times when that casual style could achieve results he doubted could be obtained in any other way.

'Like maybe you have friends in London with contacts here in Greece,' Mado said.

Andrea stood up and seemed to shake herself into a blaze of anger. 'How else does a journalist work? What's going on around here? Of course I have contacts. Who hasn't?'

'Do you suppose your contacts could find out where my wife and child could have been taken in London?'

Andrea stopped dead.

'What's that? Have they seized them as well?'

'You didn't know?'

'Do I look as though I knew it? Jesus Christ, what do you think I am? Some sort of double agent? You think I spend a week in a stinking cupboard under threat of being taken out and shot to have you start accusing me of *that*?'

'Okay, gorgeous,' Mado said with a glint at Padstow, 'you're clear with me.'

'Huh!' she said, 'since when has that mattered? And who are you anyway other than some pseudo-hippie with dated ideas on the way women react to your non-existent sexual charm?'

'Well!' Mado said, going across and putting his hands on her shoulders, 'I should keep that in for the column next week.'

He was about to embrace her when she gave him a stinging slap on the face.

'And that's for your column next week,' she said, 'don't you try that stuff on me, Mr Mado.'

Padstow smiled broadly. The military attaché looked startled and then reverted to the deadpan expression he adopted when well out of his depth. Andrea turned away.

'I'm going back to the Grande Bretagne to have a bath and clean up.'

'And then come out to Vouliagmeni,' Mado said, apparently unmoved, 'I need you to work on Marides.'

She looked sharply at Padstow.

'Yes?' she said.

'Yes, please, Andrea,' Padstow said.

'Well, tell your lecherous friend to keep his hands off me at a time like this.'

She stopped, looked at Mado and then went over and kissed him.

'It's all right, you grotty little man, I could get to be quite fond of you if I don't try too hard.'

She walked to the door and then said to Padstow: 'I have someone in London might just be able to help find Anna and the child.'

'Ah!' said Padstow, toying with a paper-knife.

'But I'll have to do it personally, if he's there. He doesn't like the telephone.'

'Oh! yes?' Padstow said. The slight inflection in the voice demanded an explanation.

Andrea hesitated and then went on quickly: 'On account of the drug scene. He's a dealer . . . with interesting contacts.'

They all thought about this for a while.

'What do you want me to do?' Padstow asked, 'book some seats on an aircraft?'

'Marides has an executive jet,' Mado said. 'We might persuade him into a package deal. Come along, gorgeous, are you really set on that bath? Or can you delay it?'

'I need a bath more than anything else in the world,' Andrea said. 'Let's be on our way.'

On leaving the Embassy for the Grande Bretagne they were followed, but in a casual way which Mado took to be merely routine, not of the kind likely to lead to another incident in the bar. At the desk, when they picked up the keys of their rooms, the clerk asked Andrea if she had had an enjoyable trip, so someone must have put over a cover story on the hotel. Her absence appeared otherwise to have been unremarked.

'Yes,' she said, 'I consulted the oracle at Delphi – a very successful experience.'

Clearly the clerk had been better informed than his innocent question suggested. However, that too could be taken as normal. Receptionists at first-class international hotels acquire a facility with the oblique and this after all was Athens. Moreover – as Mado well knew – holders of press cards do not excite suspicion if they unexpectedly stay away for a night or two. They went up to her room.

'Help yourself to a Scotch,' Andrea said, 'and chat me up with the news.'

'You could always make it as a stripper,' Mado observed, as she tore off her shirt and jeans and walked naked to the bath. 'You have some magnificent equipment stacking up there.'

She soaped herself all over, shampooed her hair and then lay in the bath, looking at him perched on the end, a Scotch in his hand.

'This is the nice part of the job,' Mado said, appreciating her splendid proportions and the unaffected smile she gave him. 'However, you'd better know what's been going on down here in the midden since you've been away.'

He gave her a résumé of what had happened in the Grande Bretagne bar and also of his meeting with Voznitsky out at Vouliagmeni.

'If Voznitsky meets you . . .'

'He'll come.'

'What are you going to offer and what do you want?'

'It's very simple really,' Mado said. 'Should Petrov really decide to defect, then inevitably Voznitsky's career is at best damaged and at worst kaput. Maybe he won't be disgraced, since even the KGB allows for bad luck, and our friend must have done exceptionally well to have reached Resident status in a Western country – but once the tumult and the shouting are over, there's likely to be a nasty blotch on the record. In the end it's the man on the spot who picks up the blame. So the Grade I dacha, the promotion to General and all the fringe benefits will be delayed, put in doubt or possibly scrubbed out for ever.'

'So he might end his days pottering about like Kruschev?'

'If he's lucky. On the other hand if he can persuade the great Doctor to see sense – I mean Soviet sense – then the blotch becomes something of a halo and he certainly has the complete answer to Ivan Karai. That one goes inquisiting back to Moscow to arrange a proper welcome for Dr Petrov.'

She got out of the bath, dried herself and put on clean jeans. Mado helped himself to another drink and watched her reflectively as she dressed. He thought it was very friendly of her to receive him in this way, although it clearly pleased her to behave as she did. But like her as he did, he still found himself wondering if there might be an ulterior motive in the way she was handling him.

'I'm sorry I misjudged you to begin with, Andrea. You're quite a girl – literally and metaphorically.'

'Well, thank you, George Mado. I'm glad we understand each other at last.'

'Why do you think they let you out?'

She paused and looked up into the distance for a second or two.

'I'm more use to them out and about and writing than stuffed away in a cupboard weeing myself with fear.'

'Who are you really working for?'

'My paper. You know that.'

'And who else?'

'You'll have to work that out for yourself – if that's what's worrying you.'

'You're a better newspaper woman than I thought,' Mado said. 'I'm not asking you to give away your sources.'

'Oh! yes you are. That's what you've been up to since we first met. It's okay by me and one of these days I might let you in a bit more. But don't try and winkle it out of me by going round the corner and laying little traps.'

'Answer me one question, though. Do you really think your friend in London can find Anna for me when all the rest of us have failed with all the resources we can call on?'

'You've spent a lifetime in security and you ask a simple question like that?'

'Yes. Yes I do.'

Mado visualised some of the action MI5, the Special Branch, the CIA and the KGB could respectively lay on when they chose to go into high gear.

'Then ask yourself what freemasonry can cut right across, through, up and down your intelligence scene – without any of you really knowing.'

'The Roman Catholic Church.'

'Not bad. A near miss,' Andrea said, leading the way out of her room. She looked as fresh as a daffodil and even Mado with every instinct negative found the sexuality disturbing. 'However, you're wrong – or rather, a little out of date.'

'All right, then, what?'

'Drugs.'

He thought about this as they left the hotel and walked to their car. He made no comment and asked no further question. When they were safely on the way to Vouliagmeni, Andrea said: 'You've never pushed drugs, have you?'

'No,' Mado said firmly, 'certainly not.'

'The drug scene defeats the lot of you professionals. I could deal, if I wanted to, in Buckingham Palace or the Kremlin – you name the place and I'd find the man I needed in a matter of hours, sometimes minutes. It's world-wide. It's the super-state of today. I'll find your Anna for you, if she's still in one piece.'

'They owe you a favour?'

'I don't answer that sort of question. I'm doing you one, though. Let's get Marides to help us out with some fast transport.'

They drove on to Vouliagmeni, followed at a distance as before. Parked near the front door of the great white house was a CD car with a turnip-headed chauffeur studiously looking neither to the right nor left.

'He's here,' Mado said, 'and I wonder who else.'

As they entered the house, Marides was standing by the main staircase in the hall, talking to Lars Sweeney, one of the American lawyers he employed in his oil business and whom Mado knew to be also connected with the CIA. They had met during the liquidation of the Tarnham connection. Indeed Lars Sweeney's activities had played a considerable part in bringing the Greek multi-millionaire to the point of actually asking Elissa to marry him. Since those events, Sweeney had prudently kept out of the way.

Like Mado, he had an acute eye for the opposite sex, and this double-edged quality called for strong self-control, especially when one's employer was a man as passionate as Marides. Mado saw the process flash up and then disappear like lightning as he walked in with Andrea, and this made him smile. Outwardly neither man gave any sign of recognition of the other.

'You go and talk to Elissa upstairs in the blue room,' Marides said to Andrea, when the introductions had been made, 'and Mr Voznitsky is waiting for you, George, in the drawing-room.'

'Is he alone?'

'No. He has Karai with him.'

'And the news on Helen?'

Marides made a slight negative gesture: 'Deal with our Russian friends first,' he said and turned back to Sweeney. Mado continued on to the drawing-room where Voznitsky, his face the colour of putty, stood stiffly by the big french windows on to the terrace, whilst Karai leant with an appearance of nonchalant disdain against the balustrade. A glance at the two told Mado all he needed to know about the interrelationship and the power structure. It was refreshing to meet such tormentors from a position of strength and in his mind's eye he remembered flashes from very different meetings in very different places.

'Good afternoon, Colonel,' Mado said, walking across and proffering his hand, 'I see you've brought a friend.'

Voznitsky shook hands as if Mado were infected. Karai walked towards them with the sort of smile Mado had seen on the faces of East End gang leaders. He affected a pungent scent and moved as carefully as a cat on the prowl.

'This is Mr Karai,' Voznitsky said, 'who is visiting Athens for the Trade Fair.'

Karai did not offer to shake hands. Like Voznitsky he

gave Mado the impression of being in the presence of a bad smell, and it crossed Mado's mind that he might be asphyxiating himself with his own after-shave.

'Well, Mr Mado,' Karai said in English, 'what have you got to say to us?'

'To you nothing,' Mado snapped back in Russian, 'so I suggest you keep walking and wait in your car. Colonel Voznitsky and I will not detain you for long.'

There was a moment of paralysis as the two KGB men digested this statement.

'I would prefer Mr Karai to hear what you have to say.'

Mado pursed his lips and did not immediately reply.

'Then it's been rather a wasted trip for both of us,' Mado said after a lengthy pause and then began walking away. Voznitsky nodded curtly at Karai who raised his eyebrows and left the room without a word and without a further glance at Mado.

'All right,' Voznitsky said when they were alone, 'now that we've met that condition, what is this about?'

'I'm prepared to offer you – and only you – access to Dr Petrov who is himself willing to talk to you.'

'No Helen Stanopoulos?'

'No Helen Stanopoulos.'

'Where?'

'You will have to put yourself in our hands for that.'

'It's not here in Athens?'

'You know that already.'

The two men stared at each other like mutually opposed frontier guards at a time of strained relations.

'You're fully protected by your diplomatic status, Colonel. You have nothing to lose.'

'Why are you making this offer to me?'

'Because you are the man concerned. I'm sure neither of

us need go into detail and I'm equally sure that we understand each other very well.'

'Then I do not comprehend what it is you are expecting
from me.'

Mado cocked his head slightly to one side and smiled.

'The British are far more generous than you give us
credit for being. Shall we say we expect nothing in return?
Let's see what happens as the result of your meeting with
Dr Petrov. After all, Colonel, you are still the Resident
here – still the man in charge.'

At that moment a tremendous explosion coming from the
direction of the hall first shook the entire house and was
then followed by the sound of collapsing masonry. The
centre wall began crumbling in a great cloud of rubble and
dust and the ceiling fell in, a huge chunk of it striking Mado
on the shoulder and knocking him to the ground. The
rumble continued for several seconds and it became obvious
that a bomb had destroyed the centre of the house.
Voznitsky, who was untouched, recovered from the initial
shock and helped Mado up from the floor.

'Are you all right?' he asked.

'I think so,' Mado said, dusting himself off, 'we'd better
see what's happened outside.'

They picked their way over the mess to where the hall
had been. Somewhere under the rubble there were people
crying for help. Karai and the Embassy driver came running in from the outside and, as the dust settled down, it
became clear that most of the middle part of the first floor
had collapsed in what at first sight seemed to be like the
bottom end of a landslide.

7

The destruction of the Palazzo Marides made the front pages of every great newspaper in the Western world. Nameless soldiers and civilians were daily shot in Ulster or Vietnam, but this had become routine. The attempted assassination of a multi-millionaire, the blowing up of his house and the unknown motives behind it shredded into pieces the fabric of secrecy with which Marides had surrounded his current affairs. It attracted not only on to him and his household but on to Greece and its regime the full glare of world publicity.

Rumours accelerated after the Greek army had finished excavating the rubble and had taken three of Marides' staff, Lars Sweeney, Elissa and the two children together with Andrea to hospital, suffering from shock and a variety of broken limbs, but had found no trace of Marides himself.

The essentials of a first-class mystery, therefore, presented themselves. Almost anything Marides did these days became instant news. This was not only because he was enormously rich and successful but also there were unanswered questions concerning his life and affairs. Was it only love or could there be a more subtle reason for his marriage to the ex-wife of the most celebrated British defector since Philby? Was it purely coincidental that the person whom the world's press were unable to find and who appeared to be the prime cause of a counter defection in the person of Dr Petrov, was none other than Marides' niece?

This blaze of publicity did not suit the Greek authorities at all. Until the outrage at Marides' house, the Greek security service had kept very much in the background. This was standard practice. The Greeks had everything to gain and very little to lose by allowing the British, the Americans and the Russians to make Athens the sort of foyer for the interchange of intelligence that Lisbon had been in the second world war.

But this hospitality depended, like Swiss banking, on a system of hermetic secrecy. The world's press was now milling about Athens to a degree and in sufficient numbers to bring highly unwelcome attention on matters the Greeks wished to keep to themselves.

'No doubt they're seizing this opportunity of servicing the equipment in Boubolina Street and taking a few days leave,' Schofield remarked to Mado and to Padstow as they awaited the arrival of Colonel Voznitsky. The cover plan had worked well. Even the Greeks, who knew almost everything else, had been fooled into thinking that Dr Petrov had been smuggled out of the country in a British man-of-war when all the time he had remained incommunicado and under interrogation in the British Embassy in Athens.

There was a sound reason for this. Petrov himself had maintained from the start that he was only asking for asylum because of Helen Stanopoulos. He did not wish to discuss his work or the allied subjects on which he was a world expert. That would be disloyal to Soviet Russia and was therefore unthinkable. But, if he persisted, why should the British bother with him at the expense of a further worsening of relations with Russia? A man on the run is one thing, a man who merely wants to stay with his girl-friend and does not have the right kind of visa is another.

'Doctor Petrov will have to learn some of the hard facts of life if he really wants to stay in the West,' Padstow had written in his report, 'but our task would be easier if Miss Stanopoulos could be ransomed or otherwise produced and brought to the Embassy for a discussion with the Doctor.'

It was the day after the explosion and Voznitsky had been invited to come to the Embassy and be prepared to travel on. Coincidentally units of the American Sixth Fleet were anchored in Piraeus harbour and so was another British frigate which had come overnight from Cyprus. Smoke screens at different levels had thus been laid. But still no news of Anna and the child in London had come in, nor of Helen Stanopoulos in Athens. Now that Marides himself had also disappeared, confusion seemed complete to the three men in the military attaché's room, as they sat drinking cups of unpleasant coffee brought to them by Schofield's pretty secretary.

'What's the current state of the casualty list?' Padstow asked. He had been keeping a careful eye on Mado, whom he thought to be near breaking point.

'Elissa and Andrea have broken legs, the children got away with facial cuts and bruises, Lars Sweeney has internal injuries and is still unconscious, and one of the servants died two hours ago,' Mado said. 'And if anyone's interested, I have a bruise the size of Piccadilly Circus on my left shoulder.'

'Have we any idea where Marides might be?'

Mado shook his head.

'The only person who might give us a clue is Sweeney, who was with him in the hall when I entered the house, and Sweeney, as I said, isn't in too good shape.'

'I think I'll send you back to London tonight, George. I don't see that there's much more for you here.'

'I thought you wanted me around for the Nevsky Prospekt?'

'Yes, George, I do. But you're obviously so worried about Anna, I don't think there's much point in keeping you hanging about in your present condition.'

'Oh! well,' Mado said, hardening his mouth, 'I don't suppose I'd be any better off in London. Her little Ladyship had the bright idea of invoking some big wheel in the drug scene but I always thought that was a far out idea and anyway if Andrea's in hospital she can scarcely do much on a long-distance basis. If the Special Branch on a red alert can't find my wife, I don't suppose there's much I can do. I'll stick around here.'

'I'm very sorry, George.'

'Thanks! I only hope it never happens to you,' Mado said and walked to the window looking out on the Embassy garden with its beautifully kept lawn. The peace and quiet seemed to counterpoint the stress bearing down on all of them at that time.

'Do we have anything new on why the explosion took place at all? And who was behind it?'

Neither of the other two rose to this and eventually Mado turned back from his study of the garden and said: 'I have nothing to go on but it wouldn't surprise me if Christos Marides was somewhere in that.'

'Yes,' Padstow agreed, 'that had occurred to me, too. He's certainly very shifty about Elissa.'

'Colonel Voznitsky is here,' the secretary said, coming into the office. Schofield and Mado followed her out to the hall. Voznitsky was standing stiff and erect near to the watchful Embassy guard, trying, as it seemed to Mado, not to breathe too much of the tainted British Embassy air. They greeted each other formally.

'Have you brought your overnight things?' Mado asked.

'Yes. They are in the car. I would also like Mr Karai to be present if that could be agreed. He, too, is in the car.'

'Ah! yes,' Mado said, 'Mr Karai . . .'

It was clear from the way Voznitsky had spoken that he was under orders to state this request. It was also clear to Mado that if the attempt to make Dr Petrov think again were to succeed, it would detract from the kudos Voznitsky could legitimately claim for his persuasive powers. Mado came to a quick decision.

'I'm sorry,' he said, 'it is only you whom Dr Petrov wishes to see.'

'Very well, but please note that I have made an official request.'

'Of course,' Mado said, 'please come this way.'

He thought he detected an almost visible relief on Voznitsky's face at the turning down of the request. The military attaché told the guard – who was an ex-Royal Marine – to keep an eye on the Russian Embassy car outside and then caught up with the other two.

'So he was here all the time,' Voznitsky said as they entered the storeroom which had been adapted to accommodate Dr Petrov, and for the first time smiled at Mado.

'We British can be damned sharp at times,' Mado said, affecting his nineteen-twenties upper-class voice which Voznitsky was not quite sure how to interpret. From then on, however, they spoke in Russian so that the linguistics were not on Mado's side. Yet to get a smile, he reflected, could be counted as some sort of achievement in the circumstances.

Dr Petrov was in a highly emotional state. The interview, which was openly tape-recorded, began in a formal way. Mado asked Dr Petrov to identify himself and to state whether he was there of his own free will or held by force. Once it was established to Voznitsky's satisfaction that, if

Dr Petrov chose, he could walk out of the Embassy there and then, a more relaxed atmosphere came about. Then the confessional began.

Although both Schofield and Mado had read reports of other defectors on whom at one stage or another the KGB persuasive technique had been brought to bear, neither of them had previously been present at such a confrontation. Mado, himself, had been interrogated several times and in depth by the Russians – once when he had been blown originally as the result of the Tarnham affair and again after he had been kidnapped in Beirut during Operation Powder Train and abducted to Moscow. But Mado had been a professional agent. Dr Petrov was nothing of the sort.

None of Mado's experiences bore the slightest resemblance to this calm, understanding, dignified discussion now taking place in the bowels of the British Embassy in Athens between the world-famous Dr Petrov and the local KGB Resident. It was one of the unwritten rules of the game that once access to a defector had been given, the host side would bring no persuasive power to bear on the defector either to stay or to return.

Even so Mado found it difficult not to jump in when Voznitsky voiced some particularly unbelievable promise. It was like watching a child teetering on the edge of a high building and not reaching out a hand to prevent a fall. But Petrov was an indoctrinated Russian professional man with no ability to strike a line of his own, with no comprehension of the real meaning – or the responsibilities of independence. He was putty in the hands of a skilful manipulator such as Voznitsky.

Moreover he was heartily sick of being out on a limb. Emotionally crippled by his obsession for Helen Stanopoulos, he believed or appeared to believe everything that this high, sympathetic and trustable officer of the state security was telling him. Mado watched the process with a kind of detached fascination.

'Wisdom and wit are little seen,' Mado murmured to Schofield at one point, 'but folly's at full length.'

'I beg your pardon?'

'I was merely quoting some eighteenth-century poet.'

'Ah! ... yes.'

'He was actually referring to an art exhibition where Beau Nash's picture had been placed at full length between the busts of Sir Isaac Newton and Mr Pope,' Mado said, and then seeing that he was making but little sense to the British military mind, went on with a glance at Voznitsky: 'Forget it. What odds would you give on Arsenal?'

'Odds on, I'm afraid.'

'Then see if you can raise a little Embassy Scotch. We shall all be needing it.'

But it was to be some time before they could decently relax over a drink. As he left the room, Schofield found his secretary about to come in.

'Mr Padstow would like to see you at once,' she said, 'and I don't think we'll be having dinner tonight.'

'Why not?' he said as he walked out.

'I'd say you'll have too much to do,' she answered enigmatically and went back to her room. These young secretaries were getting very saucy and independent, Schofield thought, as he made his way upstairs. Perhaps it was contact with the practical side of intelligence – or merely having an old ram like Mado groping his way round the place. That side of things was not on the curriculum at Sandhurst, and Schofield, like his predecessor, could not wait to get back to some active soldiering even if it meant Belfast.

Padstow was standing by the window looking at the

garden as Mado had done, when Schofield entered the room. As soon as the door was closed, Padstow said: 'How is it going?'

The question took the military attaché slightly by surprise. He had expected a panic of some kind, not just a request for a progress report.

'I think Voznitsky will persuade him to go back. My Russian isn't all that good but I gather Mado thinks so too. Was there something else you wanted to see me about?'

Schofield considered himself more experienced than this young civilian whose very presence in the Embassy was supposed, on orders from London, to be secret. He slightly resented Padstow's status and power, though he did not admit this consciously even to himself. However, the next remark put all professional jealousy out of his head.

'I've just been rung up by Marides,' Padstow said.

'He's alive! How did he manage to escape?'

Padstow shrugged his shoulders.

'He didn't waste time telling me that sort of thing. I don't even know if he's still in Greece. What he rang up to say was that we may expect Helen Stanopoulos to be delivered here at any moment.'

'Good heavens.'

'Addressed to George Mado. I only hope not as a corpse.'

'Why here? Why the British Embassy?'

'I don't know. I suppose because it's secure.'

He saw that the military attaché was not following his train of thought, so he went on: 'Marides makes a great play of his British passport – which he got through the back door in Cyprus a long time ago. Naturally he takes advantage of his Greek and Panamanian passports as well whenever it suits him. However, in times of stress he has the nice old-fashioned idea that somehow or other it's safer to be British. Regimes may come and go, bombs may explode, but the British Embassy will somehow or other always be there.'

'Well, of course he's quite right: we will be,' the military attaché said and there was no joky tone in his voice.

'Yes,' Padstow went on, 'if Helen Stanopoulos does show up, it's likely to alter the scoreboard on Petrov. I'll warn the ambassador – and that's going to help our popularity here: would you express the news privately to George? I think we ought to ease Voznitsky out of it as soon as we can.' He paused for a moment, trying to work out the implications and then added: 'Preferably before Petrov comes to a final decision.'

'I'll get down right away and pass on the gen to Mado,' Schofield said and left the room.

However, events overtook them all. Before Padstow could alert the Embassy hierarchy – the Ambassador being out on a visit and the Counsellor not available – and while Schofield was passing across to Mado a piece of paper which simply said: 'Helen Stanopoulos being brought to Embassy. Padstow suggests V asked to exit', a taxi had driven up to the front door and from it emerged, under the watchful eye of Karai and the Russian Embassy driver, the pale, limp figure of Helen Stanopoulos.

Immediately she was out, the door slammed and the taxi drove quickly away. She was alone and appeared only just able to stand. At first sight she looked either drunk or drugged and as she tottered into the Embassy hall, the guard rushed forward to prevent her falling to the ground. She was bloodless in colour and seemed scarcely able to talk, only just managing to ask in slurred tones if she was at the British Embassy.

'Yes, miss,' said the guard, whose twenty-one years in the Marines had taught him to support heavier bodies than this before, 'you're fair and square on British soil, miss.'

'Mister Mado,' the girl said with a quivery smile and then collapsed in his arms, apparently losing consciousness.

The guard, helped by a receptionist, got her to a seat and while this was in progress the Ambassador and one of the First Secretaries arrived. His Excellency had no wish for his Embassy to be used as a resting-place for sick or inebriated girls.

'What's going on?' he asked with a frown, but as no one could tell him, he passed on, ordering the First Secretary to find out what it was all about.

'She's asking for Mr Mado, sir,' the guard said and at that moment Karai entered from the porch and, with an easy smile, walked up to the group.

'Perhaps I can help?' he said in English. 'I think this is the lady who was brought by a taxi to the wrong address. We have been expecting her at the Russian Embassy. I have a car outside and can easily put things right.'

Without waiting for a reply, he leant over Helen Stanopoulos and tried to hoist her to her feet.

'I don't know who you are,' the First Secretary said, 'but thank you, we'll attend to this matter ourselves.'

'Ivan Karai – my credentials,' Karai said imperiously, producing a small wallet from his pocket.

'Thank you,' the First Secretary said, without looking at them. 'Have you an appointment, Mr Karai?'

'We were informed that the taxi had gone to the wrong Embassy,' Karai said glibly, 'so I have come to pick up this lady and take her to the right address.'

'Excuse me, sir,' said the guard, 'but wasn't you waiting for the other Russian gentleman, sir? The one who's with the military attaché?'

There was a slight pause. Helen Stanopoulos remained inert and unconscious in the chair and at that moment

Padstow appeared. He quickly took in the scene and then said to the guard: 'Escort Mr Karai to his car.'

In silence but with a nasty frown Karai turned on his heel and made for the door.

'See him *into* his car,' Padstow said as the guard hesitated near to the door. The two men then left the Embassy.

'What's going on?' the First Secretary said somewhat querulously, 'and who are you?'

'Help me to get this girl somewhere less public,' Padstow said curtly, 'and we'd better call in a doctor we can trust. God knows what they've put into her to make her like this.'

They carried her into Schofield's room.

'The Embassy doctor is Greek,' the First Secretary said. 'He's very discreet and reliable. Who is this girl?'

'I suppose there'll be a naval surgeon on board the frigate in Piraeus, won't there? Could you ask the naval attaché if he could come here at once?'

'Now look here,' the First Secretary said, bridling, 'I don't know what's going on . . .'

At that moment the Ambassador's secretary came in with a message she obviously enjoyed delivering to Padstow.

'The Ambassador would like to see you in his room right away.'

Having delivered the message, she waited. Padstow was going to have to satisfy British bureaucracy in addition to the other problems he faced. He swore silently to himself. During the pause which followed, the First Secretary said: 'I still don't know who you are.'

But there was a slightly more friendly and questioning tone in his voice, and since the timing had now become critical, Padstow took a risk. This was another of those moments of crisis when the outcome depended on the goodwill and persuasion of strangers.

'I haven't time to explain,' he said, 'but would you go

128

down to the second storeroom in the basement and ask the military attaché to come up here at once. I'll see His Excellency in the meantime.'

The First Secretary hesitated, looked at the Ambassador's secretary from whom he got no help and then set off on his mission with the pained expression of a cleric in a cathedral close to whom someone has made a sporty remark about the Virgin Mary. Padstow went in to the Ambassador, seething with impatience and before he could say a word, found himself at the receiving end of a tirade.

'I don't know what you people are up to,' the Ambassador said, 'but this has got to stop. I'm not having my Embassy used one moment longer as a sort of Harrods' waiting-room. I've been summoned to the Greek Foreign Office to receive an official complaint. You can guess as well as I can what it's about.'

'No, sir, I can't. So far as I know we've done nothing offensive to the Greeks.'

'Who's that young woman in the hall?'

'Her name is Helen Stanopoulos. She is Doctor Petrov's secretary. She is also Marides' niece.'

'It struck me she was drunk. What's she doing in my Embassy?'

'I don't know,' Padstow said grittily. 'Perhaps you could ask Mr Marides. It's cost him a million Swiss francs to get her here.'

'What's that? How do you know that?'

A scathing retort rose in Padstow's mind but he controlled himself and went on: 'And the KGB have just made one of their cruder attempts to take her out of your Embassy and into theirs.'

'Here?'

Padstow felt like telling him to belt up or wring himself out. However, he was part of the mechanism which had to be used, like it or not. He was the Ambassador for better or for worse.

'Now if you'll excuse me, sir . . .'

To Padstow's surprise, and for no reason he could discern. His Excellency suddenly thawed, rather in the manner of a self-important judge who decides he may have overdone it and that it is time he wooed the jury.

'You must find us a pain in the neck, Mr Padstow.'

'Well . . .' said Padstow. A pain in the arse is what you should have said, you pompous oaf.

'I know this is no time for apologia but I wish you people would sometimes consider the man on the spot. This sort of thing doesn't make life easy, you know, especially when you have to put up with someone like Mado.'

'If it wasn't for Mado . . .' Padstow began and then thought better of it. 'I'm sorry, sir, but I think the sooner I get back to what's going on, the better.'

'Very well,' the Ambassador said. 'I'll be leaving for the Ministry of Foreign Affairs in ten minutes' time. If you've news for me before I go, be sure I'm properly briefed.'

'Can I ask the naval attaché to get us a doctor from the frigate in Piraeus?'

'To attend a Greek girl in the British Embassy? I don't think that's a good idea. Suppose she dies on our hands?'

'She won't die,' Padstow said, an ironic twist to his mouth, 'that would be the easy way out.'

Down in the second storeroom in the basement, Mado had already decided that enough pressure had been put on Dr Petrov when the news about Helen Stanopoulos arrived. He tried to assess the effect it would have. Smootchi had long forgotten what it was like to be proud, impatient and arrogant. The confessional had reduced him to jelly, and

Mado felt something akin to compassion as he witnessed the deadliness of this self-destructive process.

It did not seem to matter whether it was operated by the Church or the KGB. It had all been done in a soft voice with gentle, suggestive words. Mado could not but admire his adversary. Voznitsky had induced the guilt into Dr Petrov and then the poison had gone racing round the veins as if he had been bitten by a snake.

But it could all be put right, Voznitsky said. Academician Petrov had made a small error in thinking – that was all. Once he came back, it would be overlooked. He could resume his life and his status as before. No one would know about his few days' folly in Greece. There might be a small enquiry on his return to Moscow but this would be a for- mality – simply to straighten the record. Everything would be all right and on that Voznitsky gave his word of honour as an officer of the KGB.

'Your time is nearly up,' Mado said to Voznitsky in English.

'For all of us,' Voznitsky replied with a wry smile. Now that he was really in action, he exhibited an extraordinary self-confidence. The resemblance to a priest, quietly exer- cising the authority of his faith, was remarkable.

'A sense of humour is a dangerous attribute,' Mado remarked casually.

'Exactly. If our friend here had had one, I shouldn't be sitting here now.'

Mado presumed that by talking in such a way, Voznitsky was either acting from bravado or taking a calculated risk. It was true that Dr Petrov's English was the minimal required to read scientific documents. It was unlikely to extend to conversational nuance. Indeed from the way he gazed from Voznitsky to Mado and back again, it was clear that he did not understand. He was like a lost dog trying to pick up a human reaction he could interpret. Nevertheless it struck Mado as a strange remark for a Russian interrogator to make in the present circumstances.

'And the outcome?' Mado asked, looking hard at Voznitsky.

'It was never really in doubt.'

'I wonder,' Mado said and decided not to let him get away with it as easily as that.

'Have you come to a decision, Dr Petrov?' he asked in Russian.

Dr Petrov went through his by now familiar routine of twitching his eyebrows, coughing and slightly shrugging his shoulders.

'I shall leave with Colonel Voznitsky.'

'Would it help to discuss it first with Helen?'

This had a bomb effect. Voznitsky tautened and Petrov almost leapt out of his skin.

'She's been found? Where is she? When can I see her?'

'I think that can be arranged.'

'Comrade Petrov,' Voznitsky said, 'remember what we've just been discussing.'

'Come, come, Colonel,' Mado said in English, 'I'm sure *your* sense of humour is more than skin deep.'

Voznitsky flashed him an angry look and then smiled.

'Are you certain you can do as you say?' he said in English, 'otherwise you are only provoking difficulties.'

Schofield who had left the room earlier on and had then come back, now whispered a question into Mado's ear.

'Yes,' Mado said, whereupon Schofield again left the room.

'I can deliver,' Mado went on to Voznitsky in English. The Russian reacted with a barely disguised sneer.

'My information is that a meeting with the girl is unlikely ever to be possible.'

132

'Where is she?' Dr Petrov mumbled in Russian, 'where is she?'

Great tears were rolling down his cheeks in a lugubrious way which was both pathetic and ridiculous.

'*Ever* to be possible?' Mado said to Voznitsky. 'That's a big statement.'

'But not made without reason, Mr Mado.'

'In other words,' Mado went on, leading him further and further into the trap, 'you have the lady under your control.'

'I did not say that.'

There was a pause as they looked at each other.

'Of course adjustments are always possible.'

'Yes,' Mado said, enjoying himself, 'you can say that again.'

At that moment Schofield opened the door and ushered in Helen Stanopoulos. She still looked pale and frightened, but at least she was now conscious and able to walk in a normal way. Dr Petrov emitted a sort of animal groan and stumbled across to embrace her. Voznitsky froze into a statue-like immobility, watched closely by Mado and the military attaché.

For a few moments while Petrov and his love exchanged more or less meaningless phrases of relief and pleasure at seeing each other again, Mado kept quiet, wondering if the ransoming of Helen Stanopoulos also meant that Anna and the baby would be released in London. Of course, he thought bitterly, that was only his personal life – a by-product of little importance. But there was no time to indulge himself in this way for long. The drama in progress in the basement of the British Embassy would have to be speedily concluded and Mado realised he must keep the initiative.

'Well, Colonel,' he said to Voznitsky, 'did I not tell you

we could deliver? Somewhere along the line your information must be at fault.'

Voznitsky inclined his head stiffly in acknowledgement. He was in a considerable turmoil, but none of this showed except for a sharp anxious look in the eyes. In fact he was completely at a loss. He had been taken by surprise, let down by his subordinates as usual. He would institute a little private terror of his own when he got back to the Embassy. In the meantime what was he now to do?

He felt a disgust in the pit of his stomach. Although he had just put up a virtuoso performance with this sentimental fool of a Dr Petrov, he could draw no satisfaction from it. He knew what would happen to Petrov when he got back to Russia. This working cynicism, for so long part of his daily life, a part he had once relished as a member of the élite, now made him almost physically sick. He became aware of being closely studied by Mado and he therefore stared back.

'You're wondering where she's been these last few days.'

'Yes.'

'So am I.'

Why was this British ex-spy being so co-operative and helpful? What sort of trap was being laid for him now? A sudden desire to be done with it all struck him with overwhelming force, so much so that to Mado's evident surprise, he sat down and in a rather clumsy way got out his handkerchief and wiped his face.

'Are you all right, Colonel?' Mado asked.

He nodded but looked away.

'Well, I could do with a drink,' Mado said, 'suppose we go upstairs – you and I – and leave Dr Petrov and his secretary together for a few moments? They'll be perfectly safe.'

Voznitsky hesitated, still on the watch for an obvious trap. Contrary to all his instinct and training, he was forced to admit to himself that he warmed towards this British spy with his pushed-in face. Indeed he not only liked him but trusted him. Once again he became aware that Mado was studying him quizzically. He managed a rather frozen smile, wondering why he felt as odd as he did.

'I accept your invitation,' he said in a formal way.

'I suggest you use the naval attaché's room,' Schofield said as they went upstairs. 'Ginger's down at Piraeus so you'll be undisturbed.'

It was important to keep Padstow out of it at this juncture.

'Look in on the lovebirds,' Mado said, 'and tell Mr P where I am.'

8

When they had helped themselves to the naval attaché's Scotch and had settled down with Mado behind the desk and Voznitsky in the comfortable visitor's chair, an atmosphere of anticipation filled the room. Like the military attaché's office, the one they were in had an agreeable view of the superbly kept Embassy lawn and garden. They might have been two leisured gentlemen in an eighteenth-century English country house, but the feeling in the air was more like that of a theatre or television studio just before the show begins.

Voznitsky thought ruefully of the contrast this deeply civilised décor made with the Soviet embassies he had known. One such embassy in which he had served had been unkindly but aptly described as an oasis of darkness in a sea of light. Once again he was compelled to admit privately to himself that it was the spirit which mattered, the spirit which gave this place its life and which so basically disturbed him.

Even though it was now a complex of government offices, the British Embassy in Athens still retained some of the elegance of the great private house which it had once been. The comparison with the furtive soullessness of his own Soviet premises filled with their ill-arranged and unloved ex-bourgeois furniture, their cracked mirrors, their seedy propaganda magazines in the waiting-room and the general imprint of prison fear, undermined yet further the wavering loyalty which was all he had left. In that sense he knew himself to be more at risk than ever he had been before, and he wondered in passing how much of this might be apparent to Mado. He did not have long to wait.

'I'm going to take a chance,' Mado said and then paused as if searching for the right words, 'I'm going to level with you.'

'I'm not sure what that means,' Voznitsky said and Mado then explained in Russian that he was going to lay his cards – or at any rate some of his cards – on the table in a spirit of trust.

'What are you expecting from me, Mr Mado?'

'Everything, I suppose,' Mado said, looking at the bronze bust of Nelson on the naval attaché's desk. And then with a shrug of his shoulders, 'Or nothing. Usually it's nothing in the experience of both of us.'

'I suggest you stop talking in riddles and come to the point.'

Mado laughed.

'I've never known a Russian yet who prefers the direct approach. But just as you like . . .'

There was another pause.

'I think I can guess what the question is going to be,' Voznitsky said, 'so perhaps it would be just as well if we approached it obliquely.'

'You see? At least it proves what I said. You're certainly a Russian.'

Again there was a pause.

'It doesn't look as if I'm going to get a lot of help from you,' Mado went on at last, 'so let me start going out on a limb. Then when I've gone far enough, you can saw off the branch.'

Voznitsky smiled. 'That allegory I understand.'

'Let me sort out the pieces and tell you what I see as the

state of play,' Mado said. 'To begin with I think you're a unique and very unhappy man. You're successful but you have a great deal – a very great deal on your conscience. This has never worried you very much in the past because your life has been spent in the company of similarly-minded spiritual cretins.'

Voznitsky realised he was being insulted but the detail escaped him. Mado saw this and checked himself.

'I'm sorry,' he said, 'but I sometimes get carried away.'

'You're trying to get me to defect, aren't you, Mr Mado?'

Mado stared at him hard, holding the pause as it seemed to Voznitsky for ever.

'But of course,' he said in a quiet voice, 'and insulting your brother officers of the KGB isn't going to help. I see that and I'm sorry. However, what I've just said is true. You are within sight of the highest range of jobs in the largest private army in the world. I salute your success. However, since you've been the Resident here in Greece, you've been finding, to your great dismay, that your heart isn't in it any more. You're an aristocrat and your life has been spent with the serfs.'

At the mention of the word 'aristocrat', Voznitsky again became completely still and as watchful as an Afghan sentry on the Khyber Pass.

'What makes you say I'm an aristocrat? Or are you simply insulting me as well as my brother officers?'

'I'm not insulting you at all,' Mado said, 'the very opposite in fact. I don't carry it around with me, but we do have a very full dossier on your great-grandfather, grandfather, father and yourself. So far as the first two are concerned we had that information before 1917 when so many records in Russia got so conveniently lost. I'm not shooting a line and I'm not trying to scare you but we do have a very detailed file on you, your wife and your relatives. We know what sort of man you are. We know most of the shameful tricks you've played. We have a long list of the people you've had shot or otherwise put away. If you were a German Nazi, you would not be alive and of course, in a sense, you have been a Nazi in spirit the whole of your adult life. Your latest victim is down below there in the storeroom kissing a fond farewell to what little he knows of a free and fulfilling life. Poor old sod! You put it over on him, didn't you, Colonel, with your very best expertise? I must say I admired your technique – and so will the wretched Petrov when you've got him safely locked away in one of your psychiatric hospitals – *if* he's allowed to stay alive. However...'

Mado poured out more Scotch for both of them and lit another cigarette: 'As I said before, you're a very unhappy man. You've begun to question yourself and that's a dangerous course of action to take. Add to that the fact that your wife spies on you and when she isn't doing that bores you to distraction . . . so you are generally disgusted with the life you have so far led. In addition you've acquired a full range of Western tastes. You even have friends – not a luxury recommended for high officers of the KGB. You've discovered you're a human being, too, like the rest of us. It all tots up to one devastating conclusion you can no longer avoid. It's simple and it stares you in the face. If you could devise some way of getting your son out of Soviet Russia, you wouldn't think twice about doing a Petrov yourself.'

Voznitsky sat very still, hardly seeming to breathe. He was mildly surprised at the accuracy of Mado's knowledge but this he could understand. He realised that the Britisher was not talking in an aggressive or provocative way. He was simply stating the facts as Voznitsky would be doing himself were the roles reversed. The extraordinary thing

139

was that instead of resenting it, he felt almost relieved. He had just applied a similar process to the man Mado described as his 'victim' and he had seen the relief flush across the old fool's face when at last it was out and the nagging, gnawing, guilt-generating secrets had been brought into the open and at least partially exorcised.

'Only one thing, in fact, holds you back,' Mado went on, 'and even of that you're beginning to be somewhat ashamed. You'd come over now – just as you are – did you not happen to have a high sense of duty – and that's the only reason you're not out of your mind.'

'I suppose I should be grateful,' Voznitsky said, 'to have one good quality admitted by this public prosecutor you seem to have become.'

Mado stiffened his approach. This was no genial chat. He had Voznitsky where he wanted him for the moment. It would be fatal to let him relax.

'Look, sport, don't interrupt me when I'm belting it out. I'm still going out on this limb. No one has yet handed you a saw. And I can get very mean and disagreeable at the drop of a hat.'

'You're surely not threatening me, are you? That would be too absurd.'

'No, no, no,' Mado said, a lightly sarcastic tone in his voice, 'no threats. Not with shiny Karai out there in the car park. Who needs blackmail when you have a man like Karai in the compound?'

'It could be that you're getting carried away again,' Voznitsky remarked in a calm voice. 'Mr Karai is merely doing his job.'

'Okay, but you're not exactly enjoying his visit.'

'He will disappear from the scene when Dr Petrov returns to Russia.'

'And that's what Dr Petrov is going to do?'

'Oh yes, Mr Mado, I don't think there's much doubt about that.'

'I wouldn't be too sure now that he's seen Helen Stanopoulos again.'

Voznitsky twisted his mouth into some sort of a smile: 'I thought you British had a sense of fair play? Was it fair to bring her in at the moment you did?'

'I'd been listening to the promises you were putting over on Petrov.'

'Well,' said Voznitsky, managing to suppress the anger he felt, 'your introduction of that particular problem will not work to your advantage. We shall require her to go to Russia as well. She knows too much of Dr Petrov's work.'

'And if she decides not to go?'

'My dear Mr Mado,' Voznitsky said, unbending into a familiarity which somehow or other did not ring true, 'you ask strangely innocent questions for a man of your experience.'

'You mean she might have to be eliminated from the scene?'

'If you were in my position, Mr Mado, I wonder how you would react?'

'Yes,' Mado said after a reflective pause, 'you're a jolly lot of thugs and murderers, you KGB.'

'Insulting us – as we said before – isn't going to advance your cause in any way.'

'Look, sport, let me make myself clear. I'm not advancing a cause. I'm doing a job . . .'

'As I am, too.'

'I carry out orders. In this case I was told to make you an offer. It's a very simple and pleasant one to make. I'm giving you the chance of opting out of it all. Whether you take it or not matters to you but not to me. Personally I couldn't care less. My only private feelings are those of disgust. Disgust and surprise that you've put up with it as long as you have. If you don't lay hold of this lifeline I'm throwing you, I shan't lose any sleep. I haven't got at least fifteen murdered men on my conscience. You're the guy with the answering to do. And you're no Karai. You don't relish what they force you to do. What's more you're intelligent enough to know that you're very unlikely to get a second chance like this. Once your present posting is over, you won't be leaving Russia again. They'll kick you up-stairs, as we say in my country, when they give out the titles and take away the power. You'll be neutered and put out to grass. Don't tell me you haven't read your *1984*. So you have some quick thinking to do.'

'You're not coolly suggesting I should defect here and now?'

'Why not? What better chance will you have?' He held Voznitsky's eyes in a cold, steady gaze. 'What *other* chance will you have? And if you pass it up, you'll never know, will you? Your life will have gone through and you'll end up as an old piece of machinery – an old car in a scrapyard – your service usefully done but with no profit whatever to your eternal soul, if you admit to such a thing . . . as I think perhaps you do.'

It was incredible. Voznitsky felt himself gulping in an attempt to suppress the emotions surging up to his throat.

'I can scarcely believe my ears,' he said in the end, and lapsed into silence. A bluebottle buzzed angrily against the window-pane and with unconscious symbolism Mado got up and let it out. Then he sat down again and stared at Voznitsky with what seemed to the Russian to be a calcu-lating smile. Around them in the immediate vicinity the daily routine of a busy Western embassy continued on its normal course. Occasionally the naval attaché's secretary put her head round the door to see that her two visitors

142

were not getting up to any mischief. A messenger brought some files and dumped them into the In basket in a casual way which would certainly not have taken place in Voznitsky's office. From time to time the sound of distant traffic penetrated the room and outside the afternoon sun beat down with a merciless glare.

'How long have you been approaching this point?' Voznitsky asked. The 'aristocratic' virus was doing its work. Mado shrugged his shoulders as if the question had no relevance.

'How would you answer such a question yourself? I'm merely the guy who puts you the proposition.'

'And what would you do if I happened to say yes?'

'Ah!' said Mado, rubbing the bridge of his nose, 'you'd have to say yes to find out.'

'I think *you* will find out that my Ambassador will shortly be calling on yours to complain that I am being held here by force. What then?'

'You would have to confront him – and your mate, Karai – and tell him you weren't.'

'And suppose I claim that I was?'

'I think we should survive,' Mado said, with an ironic smile.

'All right,' Voznitsky said, getting to his feet, 'this has gone on long enough. I am now going to leave your Embassy and I shall take Dr Petrov and Miss Stanopoulos with me.'

Mado, too, got to his feet and went to the door which he opened to allow Voznitsky to go through first.

'You may certainly take Dr Petrov with you if he wishes to go. We haven't yet discovered what Miss Stanopoulos wants to do with her life – but I don't imagine our friend Marides has ransomed the lady at a high cost just so that you can calmly abduct her to Russia.'

'So you would hold her here by force?'

'Force seems to loom large in your thinking,' Mado said, as they made their way down to the basement, 'but you know as I do the rules of this dreary game we both have to play. So be a good chap and don't provoke us too far yourself. Otherwise you'll be pushing your luck.'

Schofield was evidently glad to see them return. Dr Petrov and Helen Stanopoulos were sitting on two chairs in the corner holding hands like lovers in a park.

'Mr P would like to see you,' Schofield said to Mado, 'but he leaves the timing to you.'

'Lucky old me,' Mado said, looking hard at Dr Petrov and his secretary. 'I get all the nice decisions to take. How are you feeling?' he went on to Helen.

She compressed her lips and gave him a watery smile.

'Not very well.'

'Colonel Voznitsky is leaving,' Mado turned his attention to Dr Petrov. 'He wants you both to go with him to the Russian Embassy.'

They looked at Voznitsky who stood erect and formidable near to the door. It struck Mado that they had the dejected look of cattle walking up the ramp into a slaughterhouse and so far as Dr Petrov was concerned, exhibiting the same level of intelligence.

'You are both free to do as you please. You are both here in the British Embassy by your own choice and though I've no doubt whatever that your uncle would want you to stay here, Helen – at any rate until your mind is clear – I repeat the decision is yours.'

There was a pause. Here in this basement room lit only by artificial light, the sunlight, the embassy garden and the outside world seemed difficult even to imagine. Voznitsky said nothing. His presence was threat enough. Then slowly Dr Petrov got to his feet, and addressed himself to Voznitsky in Russian.

'You say that facilities can be provided for my secretary to accompany me to Russia?'

'I shall be delighted to arrange it. There will be no difficulties whatever. In fact it is really your duty to go.'

'Well, Helen . . . ?' Petrov said. Helen Stanopoulos gazed at him with her dark sad eyes. Then slowly she shook her head.

'I'm staying here . . . perhaps a little later . . .'

'You need not commit yourself to stay in our country,' Voznitsky said, 'you may accompany Dr Petrov as a visitor and leave when you please.'

It was on the tip of Mado's tongue to remark that if she believed that she would believe the world to be square, but he kept quiet waiting to see what she would say.

'No, thank you,' she said, 'I am not going to Russia.'

'Very well,' Voznitsky said, as if dismissing a squad on a parade ground, 'you can always change your mind. All you need to do is ask for a visa. Come along then, Dr Petrov,' he went on in Russian, 'we are expecting you to dinner tonight. My wife, as you know, makes a very good bortsch.'

'*Ne vas pas, ne vas pas*,' Helen cried in a low voice, 'I can't stand it if you go.'

She threw herself into his arms, watched impassively by Schofield, Mado and Voznitsky. With sudden and unexpected roughness, Dr Petrov pushed her away and then went over to the door.

'You stay with the girl,' Mado said to Schofield and led the way up to the Embassy hall and out into the porch. As soon as they appeared the Russian Embassy car drove up. There was no sign of Karai. As Dr Petrov got into the car, Voznitsky – somewhat to Mado's surprise – offered his hand.

'Thank you,' he said, 'I hope we shall meet again.'

'I hope so, too,' Mado said, shaking his hand and seeing

him into the car, 'my wife makes a terrible bortsch but I expect we can rustle up an egg – if I can find my wife, that is.'

'I think you'll discover she's at home in London and none the worse for the little holiday she took. Why not call her up now? Before the crisis breaks here.'

'What crisis?'

Voznitsky smiled in a foxy way.

'You don't suppose the Nikolaides will be content with blowing up a millionaire's house, do you, Mr Mado?'

'There are other treats in store?'

'Don't let your people deprive you of your diplomatic immunity,' Voznitsky said, 'in some situations it may be all you have left.'

Then, with a wave of his hand, the car drove out of the Embassy grounds.

Dr Vakelopoulos, the Embassy doctor, was a discreet man who looked after a number of embassies but who continued to hold down his job thanks to the close rapport he maintained with the security police. Because of this, his presence became a mixed blessing, his embassy clients feeling that the Hippocratic oath inevitably got itself a little bent in the process. It was inadvisable to leave him alone in a foreign embassy and now that he was examining Helen, the military attaché told his secretary to be there throughout. She had been right – they were going to be a little too busy to have dinner together that night.

Mado seized this break in the action to put a call through to London, in the meanwhile analysing the situation with Padstow.

'I don't think I did all that well,' Mado said, 'I took Colonel V by surprise – perhaps too much so.'

Padstow had been leafing through the considerable

Voznitsky file. He was fully aware of the gamble they had taken and of how little they might have to show for it at the end.

'He was expecting some sort of approach. There's always a risk with the timing and I asked you to dive in when you did. Anyway I've no complaints. A Resident is a valuable catch but if it doesn't work, it doesn't work and that's all there is to it.'

They worked back over the sequence of events they had been through in the last few days.

'I think Colonel V has a connection with the Nikolaides which we don't know about.'

'That's very likely.'

'Or he was bluffing about Helen Stanopoulos.'

'I don't think he was bluffing,' Padstow said. 'The Colonel has good underground contacts with Greek security. He'll get what help he needs in pressurising the girl. In spite of the price paid, in spite of being Marides' niece, I wouldn't rate her chances of survival as high. She knows too much.'

The telephone rang.

'Your call to London, Mr Mado,' the operator said, and to Mado's astonishment and relief, he heard Anna's voice at the other end of the line.

'Are you all right?' he almost shouted.

'We're both all right,' Anna said.

'What happened? Where have you been?'

'We were taken somewhere in the country – several hours in a car. Where, I don't know – but we're all right. When are you coming back?'

'Just as soon as I can,' Mado said. 'You were quite right – I should never have come out here.'

'Well, make it soon. I don't want another experience of that kind.'

'Were you treated all right?'

'It wasn't exactly a rest cure. But physically we're all right. We've now got police protection twenty-four hours of the day. It's a little late but it's comforting all the same.'

'Don't worry,' Mado said, 'your British police are wonderful.'

A very rude word in her native Czech impinged on his ear.

'I can tell you're all right,' Mado said, 'I'll be back as soon as I can.'

He put down the phone. A wave of relief engulfed him so that for a moment or so he felt unable to speak. Padstow poured him out an extra large Scotch.

'You can go tonight if you like,' he said, 'the Ambassador will be delighted, I'm sure.'

Mado took a long drink and stared out of the window at the Embassy garden. There was a gentle wind and above the trees the matchless blue of the Greek sky shimmered in the heat. The clarity of the light and air never ceased to astonish him and now that he knew Anna and his child to be safe, at least for the moment, he felt like taking a few hours off and going for a swim. Gradually, however, as he mastered his feelings and the Scotch took its effect, the old gambler's taste for danger returned. Padstow watched him with a smile and kept his peace.

'I said a little while back I was getting too old for this sort of thing,' Mado said eventually, 'however, I'm not too far gone not to see this thing through. I'll stick around a little longer – and His Excellency can lump it.'

'Good,' Padstow said, 'that was what I was hoping you'd say.'

9

The British Ambassador returned from the Greek Ministry of Foreign Affairs in a rare old rage which he vented at the first opportunity on Padstow. When the summons into the ambassadorial presence came, Mado said: 'I'll bet you a drachma the first thing he says is "I don't know what you people think you're doing . . ." '

Padstow frowned. 'Us people are getting brassed off with always being put on the mat simply for doing our job.'

'Gird your loins, sport,' Mado said. 'His Excellency has some other shocks coming his way. Tell him good old reliable Mado is working on the time-bomb in the basement. That'll cheer him up.'

'What time-bomb in the basement?'

'Helen Stanopoulos. Marides didn't have her sent here for fun. I'm going to have a talk with the lady as soon as Dr Vakelopoulos is through examining her. We may not have too much time.'

'I take your point,' Padstow said and went in to see the Ambassador.

'Now look here, Mr Padstow,' His Excellency said, and from the expression on his lined 'official' face, Padstow knew he had lost the bet he had just been offered by Mado. 'I don't know what you people think this Embassy is but these irregular activities have got to be brought under control. I'm not having any more of it – I don't care how many personal letters you produce from the Foreign Secretary or

149

anyone else. I've had an unpleasant and completely needless interview with the Greek Foreign Minister and I don't intend another. The Greek authorities have been very patient with us so far, but that won't continue for ever.'

'Patient – with us?' Padstow could scarcely believe his ears.

'Of course the Greeks are fully aware of the Petrov business,' the Ambassador continued, 'and, as I was forced to agree, obliged us by in no way interfering when matters reached a delicate point.'

'With respect, sir,' Padstow put in, trying not to overdo the acid, 'it suited their book not to interfere whilst the East European Trade Fair was on.'

The Ambassador did not like being interrupted. He shifted impatiently from buttock to buttock.

'Are you trying to teach me my business, Mr Padstow?'

The Ambassador glared at him with such intense dislike that Padstow made no reply.

'I am fully cognisant of the fact that your immediate chief reports directly to the Prime Minister. I realise that you are not a civil servant – nor is your Mr Mado – and that you use your constitutional position, if that is the way to put it, to suit your secret purposes. I accept the legitimacy of that. However, there is nothing in the regulations applicable to me which says that I have to enjoy your presence in my Embassy and I assure you I do not. I am also the man responsible on the spot. You come and go like fairies in the night ['Whoever told him we were queer?' Padstow said afterwards to Mado]. You suit yourselves. And you leave us to pick up the pieces and clear up the mess.'

'What pieces and what mess?'

'Well . . .' the Ambassador said, with a rather too obvious attempt to control his annoyance, 'you haven't done too well with Dr Petrov, have you? I gather he decided not to defect after all.'

'That was always his privilege. There are other equally important matters at stake.'

'The British Embassy does not exist to give sleazy little foreign dissidents the opportunity to pleasure their secretaries,' the Ambassador said. 'Nor is there any welcome here for the girl in question who, I would remind you, is a Greek citizen in her own country. That young woman is not to be given asylum here. The Greek Foreign Minister was insistent on that. They want her out of here in double quick time – and I see no reason for not complying with their wishes.'

This was a little too much even for Padstow. He decided to fight back. Disdain and exasperation were not a monopoly of the higher members of the diplomatic service. He, too, had been to Harrow.

'I was given to understand, sir, that we could look to your Excellency for all the help and support we would obviously need on our extremely delicate mission. I'm afraid the Prime Minister – through my immediate chief, as you have observed – will have to be told that things are not quite as we expected in Athens.'

'What do you mean by that?'

'Helen Stanopoulos was kidnapped, threatened with death, expensively ransomed and brought to the British Embassy because this is the one place in Athens where she might be thought to be safe. You are now proposing to show her the door.'

'Well?'

'Which is the equivalent of signing her death warrant. Why? Because the Colonels have shown a touch of steel to a foreign Ambassador?'

His Excellency was appalled. He rose slowly to his feet.

'I beg your pardon, Mr Padstow?'

'As you say, Ambassador, I am not a civil servant and as Mr Mado observed to you before we are only unwelcome visitors in your Embassy. To adapt the Duke of Wellington's famous remark: "I don't know what your Embassy does to the Greeks, but it certainly puts the fear of God into me".'

The Ambassador looked as though he might be having a heart attack.

'Luckily for all of us,' Padstow went on, 'we can call on a little more co-operation from the CIA. It's not what I want but unless you can see your way to helping us to a greater extent than you have so far, I shall be forced to arrange for Miss Stanopoulos, Mr Mado and myself to transfer to the American Embassy forthwith.'

He waited for a second or two to see if there were any signs of a change but none were forthcoming. He therefore excused himself correctly, turned on his heel and left the room.

The Ambassador sat down, overcome by shock, and then rang for his secretary.

'I shall have a pressing report for the Foreign Secretary,' he said, 'which had better go off to London tonight.'

But again events overtook them. No sooner had Padstow returned to the military attaché's office, than the naval attaché, a young Post Captain with flaming red hair and the inevitable nickname, put his head round the door.

'You'd both better come and drink some of my duty free,' he said, 'I've a piece of news which may interest the cloak and dagger department.'

As they walked along the corridor, Mado said to Padstow: 'Dr Vakelopoulos wants to remove Helen S to hospital for observation.'

'That will certainly suit His Excellency,' Padstow remarked and quickly put Mado in the picture as to what had just transpired.

'Unfortunately she refuses to go.'

'Why?'

'A little understandable Greek mistrust. She seems to think they'll "get" her once she's no longer under British protection.'

'What does Dr Vakelopoulos say is wrong with her?'

'He doesn't know, or he won't say.'

'How is she – in your own opinion?'

'Schofield's secretary says she seems to be quite all right. Whatever was put into her is obviously wearing off. As she and Dr Vakelopoulos talked in Greek, though, the secretary doesn't know what was really said. The doctor has gone, saying he'll send an ambulance for her. Apparently this produced an outbreak of the 'οχι's with a great shaking of the head.'

'I suppose she could claim political asylum, though that's the last thing the Ambassador wants.'

By this time they were in the naval attaché's room, where Ginger deftly supplied them with drink.

'His Excellency may well have to stiffen up to another situation,' the naval attaché said, 'the Trade Fair ends tonight and the word is about that the Greeks are cleaning out the stables. We all know what that means. A precautionary rounding up of any possible suspect – left-wing, liberal or urban guerilla. The Nix can always be blamed. Then comes the administration of treatment where necessary in Boubolina Street and another wave of police terror to discourage any dissidents who may still be around.'

'Where did you learn all this?'

'From my American friends. The Sixth Fleet is a great comfort in times of trouble. But that's not what I got you along for. I have a message for you from Panayotis Marides.'

'You've seen him yourself? Where is he?'

'On board one of his ships in Piraeus, a ship flying the Red Ensign,' the naval attaché said with a smile.

'You did see him yourself?'

'He asked me to visit him – all perfectly legitimate, you see, for the British naval attaché to go aboard a British ship. When I asked him why he was there, he said "Well, you can't trust the Greeks, can you?".'

'That's Pan all right,' Mado said with a chuckle, 'what's the message? What's on his mind?'

'He wants you to get his wife out of that hospital and into the British Embassy. He added that you should take Miss Eckersley along as well.'

'Why?'

'Because of what I said earlier on. The Colonels are cooking up something, and life's going to be tricky in Athens for the next few days.'

Padstow and Mado considered the implications of this and then Padstow said: 'Did he mention his son?'

'No. But I gather from my American friends that Christos Marides has had a sudden posting away from Athens.'

'Do you know where?'

The naval attaché smiled: 'I believe there was some emergency in the Greek Embassy in Moscow which he was required to take care of.'

'Or, in plain English, to get him out of the way.'

'How was Marides?' Mado asked.

'I don't know him as well as you do,' the naval attaché replied, 'he seemed to be chafing at his bit. He told me he still intends going to Pekin as soon as he can get away. I had the impression, though, that he was waiting for some-

154

thing to happen. What, I don't know. Naturally he needs to find out who planted that bomb in his house . . . and whether he was really the target . . . if he doesn't already know.'

'He'll know,' Mado said. 'It's the remedial action that's keeping him here.'

'We have some remedial action to take ourselves,' Padstow said. 'I'll get Helen Stanopoulos over to our American friends. You'd better go out to the hospital and collect Elissa and Andrea.'

'Since when has there been an Embassy ambulance?' Mado asked sourly. 'How can I do that if they can't even walk?'

'You'll think of a way, George,' Padstow said. And then with a questioning glance at the naval attaché, 'Perhaps the Royal Navy could sail in to your help?'

'I have a car with CD plates,' Ginger said with a glint of pleasure in his eye, 'let's be on our way.'

The naval attaché had been right in his prognosis of the general situation. As every service and press attaché in every major Embassy was soon to discover, the Greek dictatorship had decided on a show of strength. Not that the Colonels were insecure. Not that there was any threat to the regime. The reasons were mixed.

As Andrea Eckersley had written in one of her earlier features, the Colonels were highly successful in their running of Greece. The country was prosperous. Law and order in its outward form prevailed. Freaks and drop-outs were prevented at the frontiers from dropping in or had their hair cut and their wallets examined before being allowed to spend their money in the cradle of democracy. As under Mussolini, the trains ran more or less on time. As under Hitler, you did not argue with anyone in uniform. As under Stalin, you kept a cautious eye on the friendly stranger next to you in the bar, especially if he showed a tendency to sympathise with any criticisms you might be making of present-day life in Greece.

Why then were the road blocks suddenly manned, the uniformed police roving the streets in force, identity papers being spot checked, police cars and military vehicles rushing about Athens in a self-important way and the checking of travellers at airports and frontiers so clearly intensified? Tension was being openly and visibly stepped up by a display of force.

'Keep your diplomatic immunity,' Voznitsky had said as his parting words to Mado. 'In some situations it may be all you have left.'

Mado thought about this as he drove out to the coast hospital where the victims of the Marides house bombing had been taken, the red-haired Royal Naval captain obviously enjoying the freedom the CD plates on his car bestowed.

'Did Marides let you into any secrets as to what all this is about?' Mado asked as they passed through yet another road block, manned by arrogant-looking Greek security forces. The naval attaché shook his head.

'There has to be a display from time to time. It's part of the game. All bully boys like to show off, whether it's picketing the docks in England or tarting about like this lot here. Dictators can't live in silence for long . . . and they are the masters now. My guess is simply that there's a power struggle going on behind the scenes. Some new manipulator has gone to work. No doubt he wanted to get rid of Marides first.'

'He's such an old hand at dealing with that particular ploy,' Mado said, 'he's almost indestructible. Who do you think is behind the present gymnastics?'

'The Nix,' said the naval attaché, 'they're the only real

threat the Colonels admit to themselves. And why? Because some of the top Greek brass is in with the Nikolaides behind the scenes; because the Nix are highly organised; because they work on personal trust, they don't write things down, they avoid the telephone, they act on a nod of understanding and they take money and help from all sides without promising anything in return. They run a sort of *samizdat* of Greece. Like communists will do anything to discredit capitalism, these people act in dozens of different ways to bring down the regime. And the Colonels remain uneasy because the Nix very often know what goes on from the inside. No one is completely sure who the inside boys really are.'

'You're well informed,' Mado said.

'Well, the game began with naval intelligence, didn't it?' the captain said crisply. 'However, I don't vent that sort of remark in the Embassy. There I'm just a naval clot with ideas above his station. I can tell you, George Mado, in this appointment I've been patronised by experts.'

'I wish your Ambassador . . .' Mado began and then thought better of it. 'I suppose the little chap is just doing the best job he can by his own lights, pompous though he is.'

'Ah well, the diplomatic knows very well indeed how to be a law unto itself. That's the establishment attitude which so niggles my military colleague, Schofield. But he's more involved in it than I am. Luckily I still have a certain independence, subject of course to the Naval Discipline Act. But the Foreign Service is taking a long, long time to recover from Philby and that first husband of the lady we're going to see. Tarnham did their mandarin complex no good at all. Old pursemouth doesn't like to be reminded of that.'

'You don't seem to think very highly of our country's diplomatic representative.'

'It's a little matter of guts,' the naval attaché observed,

'and especially of not passing the buck in the Whitehall way.'

'All right,' Mado said, 'now I'll take you up on that. We've been thrown out – or rather we've just thrown ourselves out of the Athens Embassy. Now, looking at this lot . . .' he jerked his head at yet another group of ugly-looking security police who were leaning on a motorist they had stopped for interrogation, 'the timing couldn't be worse. Padstow and I need a home. The CIA can – and may have to help us out at the American Embassy. Personally I fancy something a little more British and secure.'

The naval attaché smiled.

'Well, well, well,' he said, 'now isn't it a stroke of luck that the captain of that frigate in Piraeus just happens to be a friend of mine.'

Mado showed his appreciation and pressed on: 'And suppose – just suppose I had some guests – some embarrassing guests I wanted taking care of . . .'

'A Greek girl?'

'Or the wife of a Greek multi-millionaire – a well-known woman journalist – possibly even a Colonel in the KGB.'

'You need a wholesaler, not a ship,' Ginger said, 'however I think you'll find that hospitality on board HM ships is much the same as it ever was. After all a captain of a ship is the captain of a ship. It's his judgement on the spot which really matters. The "reasons in writing" come later, don't they? It's the now that counts.'

'It's the now that matters now,' Mado agreed as they drove into the hospital grounds and negotiated yet another security check from the Greek police.

'Here is a full, detailed statement of your abduction by agents of the British security forces; your confinement against your will in an underground prison cell in the

158

British Embassy; your ill-treatment, starvation and torture, both mental and physical, together with the names of the perpetrators of this crime against human rights, notably that of the ex-spy Mado . . .'

Ivan Karai smiled at the morose expression on Dr Petrov's face.

They were in one of the interrogation rooms of the Russian Embassy, watched by Voznitsky, the proceedings as usual being recorded on tape.

'But . . .' Dr Petrov began and then stopped. He was taking a long time to accept or even to realise the hard facts of his new situation. 'That was not quite what happened,' he went on lamely.

'It is how you described it under interrogation last night,' Karai said grittily, still with that KGB smile Voznitsky knew so well and which now more than ever sickened him in the stomach. 'I should advise you to sign, Dr Petrov,' Karai went on in his smooth, friendly way. 'The matter is then adjusted so far as Athens is concerned.'

'They treated me very well,' Petrov mumbled, 'I went there of my own free will.'

'I'm afraid I didn't catch that last remark,' Karai's voice took on a sudden, steely tone. 'If you wish to add to your formal statement for the record, I must ask you to speak up in a loud, clear voice.'

'When are you arranging for my secretary to rejoin me?' Petrov said, toying with his pen but still not signing. The fool, Voznitsky thought, he still thinks of himself as the great Doctor Petrov, a power in the land. There would not be many secretaries around for him when he returned to Moscow.

'She will follow us to Moscow,' Karai said, dropping back into the syrupy tones he had used so far. 'No doubt as soon as Comrade Voznitsky has again brought his persuasive powers to bear. I congratulate you on the good sense you have so far shown, Doctor Petrov, in co-operating as you have. Now, however, time is getting short. We have a plane to catch, you and I. So if you would kindly sign that report which you have made without pressure of any kind, then, as I say, the matter is adjusted so far as Athens is concerned.'

'There will be other interrogations in Moscow?'

'Come, come, comrade, you cannot expect me to speak for the authorities in Moscow. I've no doubt you'll be asked certain questions as a result of your actions. That is natural enough. But, like this, it will be a mere formality.'

Voznitsky turned away and lit a cigarette. He felt physically sick and for a moment or two thought he was going to vomit. It was not that he could honestly express much sympathy for Dr Petrov, whose puerile lechery had brought its inevitable reward. He did not care a fig for the wobbly old fool. What was now causing him such nausea was the KGB process itself, the stench of hypocrisy in which he had lived all his life and the glimpses of dignity, honour and reasonable human behaviour he had been vouchsafed during his time in Greece.

Now in this room which, like the storeroom in the British Embassy, admitted no light of day and with its iron-bound grille could only be seen as the prison cell it was, memories of Elissa, Marides and even Mado, the ex-spy he had come to respect, rose in his mind like a cloud of ignitable gas from some jungle swamp. One match was all it needed, Voznitsky thought as he inhaled deeply, one match could blow it all up.

'Very well,' Dr Petrov said with a heavy sigh, 'I sign.'

He did so and as Karai took the document from him, the smile faded from his face.

'You will remain here until we are ready to go.'

'But . . . what about my papers? I have to pack. There are people I should thank. I have to say my good-byes.'

'All that is taken care of,' Karai said briskly. 'Your papers and clothes have all been collected. Explanations for your sudden departure have been made. In any case the Press, which made such a fuss about your attempted defection, will see to it that your return to the Soviet Union – of your own free will – is adequately publicised. Well, Colonel,' he said over his shoulder as he went to the door, 'if you have no more questions to ask, let us leave Dr Petrov to order his thoughts.'

They left the room and nodded at the waiting guard. As they walked down the corridor, they heard the familiar sound of a key turning in a lock. Part of the music of my life, Voznitsky thought, as he followed Karai into the Ambassador's room.

'Now for the girl,' Karai said with the wary look of a tiger about to pounce.

'Yes,' Voznitsky said, 'that you will leave to me, Major Karai. You have two hours before your plane leaves for Prague.'

As the naval attaché and Mado were conducted to the private wing in which the Marides victims had been put, there could be no doubt of the tension in the air. There were even uniformed police or soldiers inside the hospital, pacing the corridors in pairs or leaning with an affectation of nonchalance against the doorposts of wards which for some reason it had been found expedient to lock.

'Spend your holidays in the carefree atmosphere of Greece,' Mado remarked to his new friend Ginger. 'Even this hospital pongs of prison.'

Elissa had a large pleasant room and in one corner the boy and girl were playing Scrabble. It seemed to Mado that

Tarnham's luckless children spent their lives hanging about waiting-rooms, shielded, often inadequately, from the consequences of their father's defection and yet paying for it all the same. He was sorry for them. He had detested the father and in the early stages this had extended to the mother. Now that so much had happened since the original event, however, he found himself in a bizarre way fond of Elissa and protective of her and of the children.

She lay there in bed, looking delectable even to Mado's very different tastes. Her left leg was in plaster but the enforced rest in bed had taken the worried, strained look off her face. Or perhaps it was that, physically trapped, she had forced herself to accept the imposed relaxation with a wary humour.

'How nice of you to come,' she said, as if welcoming them to a garden party.

'You've met Captain Ericson, our naval attaché, haven't you?' Mado said. 'In any case Pan knows him and asked us to come and get you out of here.'

'I know. He told me on the phone. Things must be in a very bad way if he can't come himself.'

'The place is crawling with police. So is Athens. They must be celebrating the end of the Trade Fair and the return to a normal life. And all those nasty communists will have gone back to their own countries.'

Elissa smiled. 'With nice fat deals in their pockets done in back rooms with members of the regime.' She gestured with her hand as if brushing the whole tawdry business aside and then went on: 'I think I'll take the children home to England for a while. Since the house was destroyed, Greece seems to me an even more uneasy place than it was before.'

'Have you any idea who was behind the attack?'

'I think I can guess.'

Mado looked her straight in the eyes, 'But hasn't he had another posting?'

She nodded.

'However, his chief and his friends remain. So Pan is lying low out of caution. I think he must have identified the root of the trouble. That's why he wants me out of here and why I want myself to go back to England for a while.'

'How are the other victims?'

'The children, as you can see, are all right. The Americans have taken Lars Sweeney.'

'What Americans?'

'A naval ambulance from the Sixth Fleet came yesterday to take him aboard the flagship. He's going to need a long convalescence.'

'What about Andrea Eckersley?'

Elissa smiled. 'Can't you guess? She discharged herself yesterday just before all this police protection arrived.'

'I thought she'd broken a leg like you.'

'No. It was her arm. She looked in here before she left. I think she got one of the younger doctors to help get her out – well, he looked as if he might have been a doctor. She said to tell you, George, that as you'd obviously forgotten her existence, she had decided to remove herself before other interested parties got at her again. She said her shuttlecock days were over and you'd next hear all about it in the columns of the *Sunday Expectorator*.'

'Which arm was broken – the writing one?' Mado asked. 'Andrea can look after herself. You're the one who obviously needs some help. How soon can you be ready to move?'

'In about ten minutes,' Elissa said, 'but you may – we may have a little trouble with the staff.'

10

Dusk was settling over an Athenian day in which inner and outward confusion had slopped over the scene like storm water over marshy land. To unspecialised eyes the show of force which the Greek authorities were making remained discreet. It was high summer. Athens still bulged with tourists and the dictatorship had by now become expert in applying pressure only – or more or less only – where it suited the purposes of the moment.

The tourist board and the business community of Athens had long been anxious – indeed at times desperately anxious – to improve the tarnished image of Greece as a free country where the life was all the time improving in quality and where any political restrictions could be depicted as purely temporary but necessary measures to achieve specific ends.

Secrecy, of course, remained an essential cloak over what really went on at any particular time and when that cloak had to be drawn aside, as in the current show of force, it was done as tactfully as possible so far as foreigners were concerned.

Outwardly, therefore, in the streets of Athens there was overt control but no paralysis. Traffic bustled about more or less as usual. Certainly identity checks were being carried out but no one was manhandled. No one was hindered from goofing at the Parthenon nor from swigging ouzo in the cafés of Constitution Square.

In so far as foreign embassies were concerned, the daily

routine had gone on without interruption. Appointments were made and kept, people came and went and, in the British Embassy, no visitors and few of the staff were aware of the strange events connected with Dr Petrov, nor of the carry-over effects on a white-faced Greek girl now sitting unhappily in the leather armchair in the military attaché's office.

By now the ordinary working day had come to an end. No one remained in the Embassy except the duty officer, the guard and the few officials who wished to dispose of their paperwork after hours. Even these drifted away in ones or twos until only Padstow, Schofield and Helen Stanopoulos were left. Outside in the darkening garden, a little evening breeze moved in the trees: otherwise the Embassy had been put to bed in its normal way.

'You want to get rid of me, don't you?' Helen said to Padstow and Schofield, 'Why?'

'Because you are a Greek girl working in Greece for the United Nations. Because you have recently been the secretary of a controversial Russian specialist. Because your uncle is embroiled in Greek politics and the local urban guerillas have just used you as a bargaining counter. All that adds up to an embarrassment to us or to any foreign embassy,' Schofield said. 'And now that you have refused the ambulance Dr Vakelopoulos sent, there are bound to be repercussions.'

'You say my uncle had me ransomed and sent here: then why doesn't he come here and collect me himself?'

'He may be in danger himself. Not maybe but obviously is,' Padstow said, looking down on the colour dying out of the hibiscus and bougainvillaea in the Embassy garden. In spite of the quiet evening, he felt a growing unease as if some jungle animal were prowling in the undergrowth out of sight but nevertheless very much present.

It had been on just such an evening some years before that Rupert Eynsham had been shot, an early by-product of the Tarnham connection, and now the wheel had turned once more – or was it a spiral and not a wheel? Not that it mattered. Tension, not philosophy, dominated him now. He turned back from the window as Helen Stanopoulos spoke after a pause.

'My uncle has led a dangerous life, but he is a man the Colonels respect and admire. He is powerful and rich.'

'Then why are you so afraid?' Padstow asked gently.

'I am not my uncle. I'm just me.'

'But you can't stay in the British Embassy the rest of your life. You're not even a Hungarian cardinal,' Padstow said with an unsuccessful attempt at a lighter touch. As the evening deepened into darkness so did this feeling of nervous pressure, of some great unknown danger looming over their heads.

'I don't know what to do,' Helen said simply, staring at her feet.

'It's about time we heard from Mado and Ericson,' Padstow remarked to the military attaché, and at that moment Mado walked into the room, taking the stage so to speak, and reopening their connection with the outside world.

'What are you glowering about?' Padstow said.

'I've a lot to glower about, I suppose,' Mado replied and gave a brief smile at Schofield, who, in an almost automatic reflex, poured him a sizable Scotch. Then Mado turned on Helen and gave her a clinical look.

'I'm glad *you're* still here at any rate,' he said. 'Are you all right?'

She nodded in a glum way. Mado took the drink from Schofield and then walked to the window to stare down into the garden which was now a dark, shapeless mass.

'Well, George, you're certainly building up the anticipation. We're all of us agog. Where is Elissa? And if it comes to that – where the white hope of the Sunday press?'

'Andrea got away and out of it before we arrived,' Mado said. 'Elissa and her children are being held in the hospital by force. There's an armed guard on them all. They refused – after a little tapping of revolvers – to let us remove them into our CD car.'

'Where's Ginger?' Schofield remarked.

'He dropped me here and then went on to see Marides.'

'What's your interpretation?' Padstow asked. Mado shrugged his shoulders and paused before answering.

'The simple one would be Greek red tape – which is certainly in it anyway. The officer in charge told us that Mrs Marides and her children were being kept where they were for their own safety. He obviously believed what he had been told. Those were his orders and I don't think he knew much more about it than that. Conceivably it's true and justifiable. The name Marides certainly carries its usual impressive weight. The security officer was in awe of it and was only doing what he was told. He quite evidently felt awkward and afraid but there could be no getting round him – diplomatic status or not. There she was and there she stays. Frankly I think they're after Marides himself. We're into yet another of the Colonels' internal razzamatazzas. Marides and his son are both deeply committed . . . not necessarily on the same side.'

'A sort of local King Lear situation?'

Mado nodded.

'Except that Pan will never let himself be caught like the hoary old king. He has a high sense of self-preservation. What would you say to that, Helen?' Then, without waiting for her to answer, went on: 'Marides is more than a

match for the Colonels en masse – or en Mafia if you like –
just so long as he stays alive.'

He paused and then, watched by Padstow and Schofield,
walked over to Helen and perched himself on the arm of the
chair next to her.

'I have a feeling you could help us very much more than
you have so far,' he said, 'of your own free will.'

He looked at her hard so that she turned away uncomfortably.

'Without ideological pressures – even if you are any one
of the dozen different breeds of communist – which I somehow doubt.'

'Why should I help you?' she said with an irritated toss
of the head. Mado shot an amused glance at Padstow who
was studying the Greek girl intensely.

'You Greeks really have *hutzpah*, haven't you? I'll tell
you, Helen Stanopoulos, why you should help us – because
you're sitting safe and sound in the British Embassy where
no one is going to do you any harm. Because if we throw
you out, as our Ambassador has told us to do, there are
two things likely to happen to you. One is that you will be
abducted all over again by your Russian friends and the
other is that you will be tactfully and quietly killed. You
want to bet on it?'

He paused, expecting a reaction, but rather surprisingly
none was forthcoming.

'You know too much, you've made a proper fool of yourself and of all of us by your affair with Dr Petrov. Now
that he's let you down . . .'

'He hasn't let me down.'

'I don't see him around. If he really loved you, wouldn't
he have stayed?'

'That's not fair. He . . . he didn't want to be disloyal to
his country.'

'All right, Helen. We're not writing the front page of a newspaper. Let's say he's not disloyal. But you love him – why don't you follow him to Russia?'

'I very well might.'

'Knowing what is likely to happen to you there if you did?'

'Yes,' she said, looking down at the floor. 'Even though I am very afraid.'

'Your ex-boy-friend Nikos – if that's his name, but you know who I mean – he's the key to it all, isn't he? He's the one the KGB pays, he's the one who can talk – softly or loudly – to Mr L or whichever of the Colonels' gang is currently playing the Heinrich Himmler part. He's the one who organised your abduction and your subsequent release – the one who put it over on me in the Grande Bretagne bar. He's the one we really have to deal with, isn't that so?'

'I think so,' she said, 'but I'm really not sure.'

'What does Nikos and his – what do the nickerboys want?'

'I don't know.'

'I think you can make an informed and intelligent guess. They've got Mr Lycopoulos his million Swiss francs. They've had their six comrades released. What are they after now?'

'I really don't know,' Helen said and at that moment the telephone rang. Since they were in the military attaché's office, Schofield, on a nod from Padstow, picked up the phone.

'Of course – put him through,' he said and then identified himself to the caller at the other end. 'Yes, it's Dick speaking . . . WHAT? . . . Good Lord . . . what are you going to do? Sorry, that's a silly question . . . I know . . . well, thanks for the call. I'll drop round and see you later on.'

He put down the phone.

'I think I must ask you to wait next door, Miss Stano-poulos,' he said, 'I have something to discuss here in private.'

She got up and followed him into the naval attaché's room where, after he had given the room and the desk a brief security check, he left her and then returned to the others.

'That was my opposite number in the American Embassy,' he said. 'Two of the Soviet cypher clerks have defected. They went to the American Embassy and asked for political asylum. As you know, the Russians never let out any of their key Embassy staff alone – there's always one watching the other – well, this time the pair of them, the watcher and the watched, have done it together. My colleague thought it might be of interest to us with the current problems we have.'

'I'd whistle,' Mado said, 'if I could find the breath.'

'Colonel Voznitsky really isn't having a nice time at all, is he?' Padstow said with a huge grin. 'My heart bleeds for the KGB.'

'What happens now?' Schofield asked, as if talking to himself.

'It could do the trick,' Mado said, sucking on a tooth reflectively. 'Voznitsky can possibly survive not getting that Greek lovebird to follow Dr Petrov to Moscow: but two more defections by vital Embassy personnel . . . I should think that signals his instant recall.'

'And if that happens, he might just decide to make the break.'

'The point is do we wait for him or do we go out and get him?' Mado asked and immediately regretted it.

Padstow smiled at him: 'I think you might go and get him, George.'

'Thanks. Just walk into the Russian Embassy and ask him to follow me out? *How* do I get him?'

'Just go and get him, Georgey,' Padstow said. 'You have your diplomatic immunity and all that lovely charm.'

'You mean it, don't you?' Mado said incredulously. 'You think I'll do anything to get myself in shtuck, don't you? Well – this time – no!'

'It's what you came here to do.'

'There's that little matter of provocation – remember?'

'As we're not personae gratae in our own embassy,' Padstow said, 'I think we can drop that one out of the top twenty.'

Almost as if they had been overheard, the duty officer knocked and entered the room. He hesitated a moment, wondering whether to speak in front of them all and then said to Padstow: 'I've just had a phone call from the Ambassador. His Excellency asked if Miss Stanopoulos was still in the Embassy and if so I was to ask you why?'

'And what did you say?'

'I told him she left five minutes ago.'

'Thank you,' Padstow said. 'It's very good of you to front for us in that way.'

'But she did leave five minutes ago.'

'What?'

The three intelligence officers froze and concentrated an abrasive, disbelieving stare on the duty officer.

'She simply walked out. I thought you knew . . . I mean . . .'

The duty officer faltered into a numbed silence. He had only been in the Foreign Service a couple of years and this was his first foreign posting. The military attaché, Padstow and Mado looked at him so intently that he felt like a piece of cellophane melting in a fire. A total silence took possession of the room.

'You don't get a lot for a million Swiss francs these days, do you?' Mado remarked casually. The funny side of it struck him so that he had to turn away to hide a smile.

'I . . . I didn't know,' the duty officer stammered. 'Wasn't she free to leave?'

'Oh yes,' Padstow said, 'free as the air. After all this is British soil. We don't have a KGB. We don't hold anyone by force . . . Christ Almighty,' he said and then realising it was pointless, went on: 'well, I'm glad you set the Ambassador's mind at rest. Thank you.'

He nodded a dismissal and the duty officer left in a crestfallen way.

'Any more Scotch in that bottle of yours?' Mado asked Schofield. 'It's turning a little chilly for August, isn't it?'

If the Soviet Embassy, on Dr Petrov's departure, had been like an ant-heap on which boiling water had been poured, it now resembled a town facing the lava stream from an erupting volcano. The whole building became fear-haunted to the point of a paralysing panic.

No one knew what would happen next but it was certainly not going to be 'kulturny'. Voznitsky had had the building sealed. No one could leave even for normal rest and recreation until further orders. He had already applied the first investigation process ordered by the regulations. The defectors' immediate superior was under arrest. The news had been immediately passed to Moscow since the two cypher experts had taken with them the current key codes to an important part of the system.

Voznitsky had just finished briefing his Ambassador for the calls he would have to make on the Greek Ministry of Foreign Affairs and the American Embassy, when Mado rang up.

'You're a very difficult man to get through to,' Mado

said in Russian, knowing that everything said would be recorded.

'What do you want, Mr Mado?'

'I wondered if you were free for a drink.'

'I'm sorry. I'm not available.'

'Even if I have some interesting news about Helen Stanopoulos?'

'What news?'

'You would hardly expect me to tell you on the phone.'

'I can see you for a minute or two if you come to the Embassy.'

'Thank you, Colonel. My last visit to Russian soil turned out unhappily. I shall be in my room at the Grande Bretagne in half an hour's time. I shall hope to see you there.'

Voznitsky put down the phone and looked at the picture of Lenin which faced his desk. He had always secretly detested the crafty look on the little father's vole-like face. Now he found it almost unbearable and it was all he could do not to get up and turn the picture to the wall. It was just as well, however, that he resisted the temptation since a moment or two later his wife came into the room.

'I have not been able to contact Nikos Nikolaides,' she said in the military tone of voice she used when on duty. 'He did not attend the rendezvous.'

'See if you can produce some more good news,' he said sourly, 'then we can open the champagne.'

'You talk like a Western decadent,' Irina said, unable to keep out of her voice the haughty power which he knew she possessed. It was an unwelcome reminder that he, too, was under observation twenty-four hours of the day. Such softness as she had ever exhibited in the privacy of their home was totally absent now in the KGB officer whose job was to watch and report on her husband. Voznitsky's stomach heaved as he looked at his wife.

'It's high time we went back to Moscow,' she said, an unexpected break in her voice, 'this kind of life is not for us, Alexei. It results in what is happening now – and that is not good for either of us, and least of all for Boris.'

Suddenly and to his distress and embarrassment, she began to cry. She stood quite still in front of his desk in the correct stance a subordinate should adopt in the presence of a senior officer – even if that officer were her husband – and the tears coursed down her face. He got up and put his arms round her thick, sturdy shoulders.

'Don't cry,' he said, 'it has all happened before and it will do so again. It is not our fault. How can it possibly be our fault?'

'We should never have come to Greece,' she cried, 'it was all a mistake. We are better off in Russia, Alexei. Ask for us to go back as soon as we can.'

'I don't suppose that will be necessary,' he remarked drily and nodded at her to go, 'I should think we will be recalled just as soon as Karai or some other ambitious young tiger can be sent back to Athens.'

Not that George Mado set off for his assignment in any benign frame of mind. Although neither could know it, both Mado and Voznitsky stood in a somewhat similar relationship to their respective establishments. A few minutes before Mado left the British Embassy an urgent Top Secret telegram had been handed to Padstow by the duty officer. It was from his chief in London.

'Strongest representations have been made by Ambassador Athens requiring cessation all special operations forthwith plus withdrawal diplomatic privilege Mado stop Had Petrov co-operated pressure could have been resisted stop

However in default positive results Operation Resident must now be regarded as cancelled stop all personnel return London earliest.'

'A great message of good will,' Mado commented as he drained the last drop of Schofield's Scotch and prepared to leave for the centre of Athens. 'The General addressed his troops on the eve of battle,' he declaimed, striking a Napoleonic stance, 'and told them not to worry too much about the enemy, they would all be shot in the back in any event.'

He had decided to walk. This would irritate the car-borne trackers put on to follow him and it would also generate a certain local uncertainty as to what he was minded to do. He knew he would be followed, and he also knew that Schofield would be following the followers. Picturing this somewhat ludicrous process as he walked gave him a brief exhilaration and made him smile. There was very little else to amuse him in the prospect before him.

Mado did not hurry. What was there to hurry for? If Voznitsky had decided to defect, he would do so now without further pressure from Mado. He could wait. If he were only trying to find out some news about Helen Stanopoulos, then the aggravation this would provoke could well be delayed. Mado felt an old familiar calmness steal over him as he walked. This was always an indication of danger in the offing. Exactly what danger he did not know nor did he attempt to analyse the form it might take. Mado had been too long in espionage not to appreciate how comparatively unimportant were the lives of individual operators. He had survived so often in similar circumstances only by the grace of God. Now he had the full fatalistic approach to what remained of his life. He wondered if Voznitsky had reached the same point of understanding. Not that it mattered. *Que sará, sará.*

175

He collected the key of his room at the Grande Bretagne and went upstairs. Everything appeared to be in order. The few papers in his brief-case had again been sorted through and inspected for the umpteenth time but as they contained nothing of value, this was, if anything, an indication of normality without sinister overtones.

He walked over to the window and looked down on the centre of Athens. It struck him that there were fewer people than usual bustling about Constitution Square but no doubt the news of the current security blitz had been spread about. Such rumours ran round the Greek capital like quicksilver and were always acted upon. The Greeks had become expert at going to ground when trouble seemed in the offing and to know what was happening slightly ahead of the arrival of a security squad might well be the difference between survival and the usual treatment. The Greeks were no fools, Mado thought, as he watched a youth dodging an identity check whilst a girl-friend distracted attention. They had learnt a thing or two from the Turks in five hundred years.

'Well, Mr Mado, are you enjoying your stay in Athens?'

He spun round to find himself being addressed by a complete stranger who had either entered the room noiselessly or had been there, in hiding, when Mado himself had arrived. The man was heavily built and affected dark glasses so that his eyes were invisible. He moved, in the way Mado had trained himself to move, with an easy stealth so that 'cat-like' was an apt rather than a merely trite description of the stranger. He was expensively dressed and his thick sensual lips gave him a cruel, sardonic expression. Not a nice man, Mado thought, to find in your room uninvited at a time like this.

'Who are you? And why are you here?'

'I am Mr Lamda,' the stranger said and smiled as the

effect of this sank in. Mr L's smile was one of the nastiest Mado had seen in years. 'As no doubt you know, I am the one who usually asks the questions.'

His English was excellent and as if reading his thoughts, the Greek went on: 'You are wondering how I speak such good English, Mr Mado. I will tell you. My mother was English and I went to an English school.'

Mr L was clearly enjoying himself and his attitude reminded Mado of Panayotis Marides whenever he chose to be in one of his cruelly playful moods.

'I know who you are,' Mado said and stared back at the dark glasses. He supposed that the chief of the Greek Gestapo wore such glasses in order to increase the fear his appearance induced.

'Why are you here?' he went on as Mr L did not seem disposed to talk.

'I have one or two matters to settle in a quiet place. What better than in the room of a visiting diplomat in the Grande Bretagne?'

'Matters to settle with me?'

The smile broadened: 'No, Mr Mado, you can relax. You were sent here as "bait" were you not? Well, I am a fisherman, too. It is the people coming to see you who interest me.'

'People? I'm only expecting one man.'

'There may be a bonus.'

'All right, Mr Lamda,' Mado said cheerfully. 'Would you care for a Scotch before the curtain goes up or shall we order our drinks for the interval?'

'Thank you. I neither drink nor smoke.'

'Lucky old you,' Mado said, helping himself to a drink, 'and I bet you've a tidy little nest-egg put away as a result. Like a million Swiss francs, for example.'

Mr L showed no sign of reacting to this. He sat down

delicately in an armchair and peered, stared or glared through his dark glasses at Mado. It was impossible to gauge what was going on in his mind.

'Ah! yes, money,' he said, 'and what is your interest, Mr Mado, in following the occupation you do?'

'I've been asked that question a number of times in a number of different ways.'

'Try answering it then.'

There was a soft, soft threat in the voice. Mado did not reply.

'Isn't it primarily money?'

'Yes,' Mado said, watching the other acutely. 'We all need money. Why do you ask?'

'I am a student of psychology.'

Mado suddenly realised that Mr L had a small gun in his hand. He had not seen him take it out of his pocket and he was not threatening Mado. He simply had it in his hand, resting on his knee as if it were the most natural thing in the world.

'I'm surprised Mr Lycopoulos finds it necessary to go about armed.'

'You have several surprises in store, Mr Mado.'

'But surely your presence here means that there are security guards festooned round the place.'

'Sometimes I prefer to work by myself.'

The telephone rang and the hall desk informed Mado that he had a visitor.

'Send him up.'

'I will wait in your bathroom,' Mr L said, putting away the gun, getting up and going across the room in one continuous movement.

'I'll be sure to shout if I need any help,' Mado said with an attempt at a joke. He felt more coldly in danger than ever before, without knowing why. Whilst waiting for

Colonel Voznitsky to arrive, he tried to work out the real reason for the presence of Mr L and in what way it could affect the proceedings. What was he doing there at all? And why had he made a display of being armed?

A shiver went down his spine as the door opened and instead of Voznitsky whom he had expected, Andrea and Nikos Nikoladies walked into the room.

II

It struck Mado at once that although Andrea appeared to be carrying on in a normal way, she must nevertheless be there under some form of duress.

'Surprise, surprise!' Mado said, glancing quickly at the Greek's right hand to see if he, too, was armed, and then at the smiling face.

'You would expect me to be, wouldn't you, Mr Mado?'

'What can I do for you now?'

But it was Andrea Eckersley who answered: 'Colonel Voznitsky is on his way here. Nikos wants a word with him too. That's why I brought him along. He helped me get out of that hospital yesterday.'

'I think Colonel Voznitsky is expecting to find me alone.'

'The Colonel is used to quick alterations of plan,' Nikos said.

'None the less, if it's all the same with you,' Mado said, 'I would like to talk to the Colonel all by myself. Perhaps you could wait in Miss Eckersley's room next door – or in the bathroom.' He turned away to suppress a smile. It was a nice idea to put them all in together.

However, events moved too quickly for any of them. The door opened and Voznitsky walked into the room, stopping dead in his tracks on seeing the young Greek guerilla leader. Then he turned to go out.

'No, no, no,' Nikos said, 'now that you're here, you must stay.'

Voznitsky paid no attention but continued to the door. When he had his hand on it and was about to open it, Mado said:

'He has a gun, Colonel.'

'No doubt,' Voznitsky said contemptuously, 'but he won't use it here.'

He had scarcely finished speaking when Nikos put a shot into the door a few inches away from his hand. He had been telling the truth, Mado thought, in the Grande Bretagne bar – the low-calibre pistol made very little noise and was obviously an effective close-range weapon.

Voznitsky turned in a dry rage: 'How dare you?'

'How dare *you* not honour your side of the bargain?' Nikos said, equally coldly. 'You owe us a great deal of money.'

'You did not deliver.'

'Mr L is no longer around. He has been taken care of. Tonight he will be officially replaced as head of special security by one of us – with the regime's concurrence. What else were you expecting us to deliver?'

'You tricked us over Helen Stanopoulos. You traded her to the British.'

'That was where Mr Marides wanted her sent.'

There was a slight pause and Mado said: 'But surely, Colonel, that is why you are here now?'

Voznitsky turned and looked Mado straight in the eyes: 'No, Mr Mado. I am not here to find out anything about Helen Stanopoulos. I have no need to. She has come to the Soviet Embassy of her own free will and has asked for a visa. She wants to join Dr Petrov in Moscow and so, of course, arrangements are being made. No, Mr Mado . . . I have come here to see you.'

'Ah!' said Mado and smiled with his eyes. 'I understand.'

There was a pause, during which Mado digested the

news. There could be only one conclusion to draw. Voznitsky was about to make the big jump.

In the event the Resident's decision looked so simple that all the complications which had previously hedged it in now lay scattered about in bits. But if it were as simple as it now appeared, why had Voznitsky not gone straight to the British Embassy? Why risk it a moment longer on so-called 'neutral' ground? Once again warning bells began to ring in Mado's mind.

'In the meantime where is the money you contracted to pay us?' Nikos went on relentlessly. His gun still covered the Russian.

'You have already been paid.'

'Only fifty percent. Come, come, Colonel – don't waste my time. We know the money is there. Only the transfer form needs to be signed. You don't really think you could shortchange us on a matter of this size, do you?'

'It will be paid tomorrow when Mr L's disappearance is definitely confirmed.'

'Yach!' Nikos said, 'you are playing with words. If *I* tell you Mr L has gone, you know quite well it is true. You already accept that we really control Athens, Colonel. You know that I have only to give the order and you yourself will disappear from the scene until the matter is settled . . . or you could disappear for ever.'

That, no doubt, was what the Colonel intended to do in another sense, Mado thought ironically, as he now watched the intimidation process being applied to someone expertly accustomed to handing it out himself.

'Why are you threatening me?' Voznitsky said, 'I don't carry the transfer form around in my pocket. Also you did not come to the rendezvous as arranged: you could have had the transfer then.'

'That is merely a stupid lie,' Nikos said.

'We asked you to *eliminate* Mr Lamda,' Voznitsky said.

'Your people must have checked that he has disappeared. He is no longer around.'

'A temporary disappearance is not the same as elimination,' Voznitsky said, 'proof is required before the final payment is made.'

'Proof? What proof? Do you want a sight of his scalp?'

Once again Mado tried to cool it: 'But surely that doesn't concern you any more, does it, Colonel?'

Before he could answer, the door was flung open and Marides strode into the room, stopping abruptly as he took in the scene. Almost lazily Nikos ordered him in Greek to put up his hands.

'I don't carry a gun,' Marides said with the greatest contempt. 'What is all this play-acting about?'

'No play-acting,' Nikos said, gesturing with the gun. 'Simply a trap – and you've walked into it. You should never have left your ship.'

Marides laughed in that dangerously mirthless way Mado knew so well.

'You're not seriously trying to put this over on *me*, are you?' he said. 'You failed when you blew up my house, you don't imagine . . .'

'I should do as he says, Pan,' Mado remarked quietly, 'he's a very trigger-happy young man.'

'And you keep out of it,' Nikos snapped to Mado, 'your part in this matter is over.'

He signalled to Marides with his gun and with a look of incredulity on his face, Marides raised his short, thick arms above his head.

'You must be crazy,' he muttered.

'Not at all,' Nikos said with a smile, 'you came here expecting to find Mr Lycopoulos but Mr L has already been removed from office. By tonight the rest of his particular clique will have been disposed of and we shall then control the situation outwardly as we now do behind the scenes.'

Nobody moved in the room. Now everyone realised that although Nikos Nikolaides might well be foolhardy – perhaps even mad – he certainly meant what he said and had the means in his right hand of imposing his will.

Mado glanced at Andrea and tried by a jerk of his head to get her to go to the bathroom, but this signal was intercepted by Nikos who said sharply: 'No one moves. Everyone stays where they are.' Then with a brief look at Mado he added: 'And you can join the others over there with your arms above your head.'

'I might spill my whisky.'

'No funny jokes,' Nikos said curtly.

'My jokes never are funny,' Mado said and moved across as ordered. Out of the corner of his eye he saw the bathroom door open. Nikos had his back to this door and was watching Mado move across when everything seemed to happen at once.

On a sudden impulse Mado hurled his whisky glass hard at the guerilla's head. This missed but shattered a mirror on the wall behind. At the same time Nikos fired at Mado, grazing his inner thigh, but a moment later himself crumpled up and fell to the floor, having been shot three times through the spine by Mr L. Voznitsky decided to get out as soon as he could and wrenched open the door but found himself gripped in a tight bear hug by Marides.

'Stay a little longer,' Marides said and with a quick jab swept his legs from under him so that Voznitsky fell to his knees. 'You've some questions to answer.'

'In any case,' Mr L said, calmly walking across to look at the dead guerilla leader, 'you wouldn't get far.'

The room now began to fill up with security police. Andrea, who had been crouching for cover beside the bed, came across to where Mado had fallen and helped to get him up on the sofa. His leg was bleeding but it was only a flesh wound on the top inner groin, the bullet having missed its vital mark by a couple of inches.

'Are you badly hurt?' she asked.

'I don't think so. Not where it matters. Get some towels from the bathroom and bind up my leg, would you?'

Very much shaken, Andrea did as she was asked. In the meantime Mr L had gone over to Voznitsky and ordered him to stand up.

'Your diplomatic immunity is not going to help you now,' Mr L remarked. 'I intend having a full report from you in your own words of every transaction you made or were planning to make with this young man – especially my own removal. I think we can help you make this report at police headquarters and I'm sure you know what I mean by that.'

He nodded at two of the security police, who dragged Voznitsky to his feet and took him out of the room. Then Mr Lamda walked over to Mado, whose wound was being bound up by Andrea and Marides. When this was done, Mr L continued his apparently sightless gaze at Mado.

'Your help was vital and Greece will thank you for it,' he said with acid politeness, well aware of the way this remark would be received.

'I don't collect medals,' Mado said, 'at any rate not from people like you. I just like staying alive.'

He broke off to watch two policemen carry out the dead Nikos. Then he looked over to see where Andrea had gone. She was now sitting on the bed trying to control a fit of shivering which had overcome her. Mr L watched them both through his dark glasses, an impassively calculating expression on his face. Mado had to remind himself consciously that Mr L had just killed a man in front of his eyes. Anything could happen in Greece these days.

185

'However, I think it would be advisable for you to stay away from Greece, Mr Mado, even if you do change your employment.' Mr L glanced at Marides as he said this, but Marides was adjusting his tie and brushing off his suit. 'It is none of your business how we run things in Greece. I know you came here for a different purpose and then found yourself involved. Nevertheless you will not be a welcome visitor here for some little time.'

'Is that how Greece thanks me for my "vital help"?' Mado stared back at the dark glasses and, as always, attacked when he thought he had the advantage. 'How about trading me the Colonel,' he said, 'once you've got your report. Then we can call it quits. You give me Colonel Voznitsky, preferably not too badly shopworn, and I'll stay away from your country for as long as you like.'

'You certainly live up to your reputation of nerve,' Mr L said coolly, 'or perhaps I should say impertinence.'

'What are you going to do with the Colonel then? When you've finished your personal vendetta?'

'That will be for the military tribunal to decide. Probably give him back to the Russians. They know how to deal with people who fail.'

'You can't brush aside his diplomatic status just like that.'

Mr Lycopoulos smiled and made a little chewing movement with his lips.

'Can't we?' he said. 'I think you'll find that we can. Mistakes are always being made . . . and of course apologies can always be given at a later date. In any case we shall have a very full admission of the facts – which the KGB may well wish to suppress – and that will be enough. But you are right in one respect,' he shot another glance at Marides, 'there will be reprisals on our own diplomats in Moscow. I'm afraid Christos may find things a little difficult for him there. After all he and Nikos Nikolaides were close associates, were they not, Panayotis?'

'I know nothing of that,' Marides said curtly. He had finished repairing his appearance and was now intending to get on with his ordinary life without further delay. 'I take it I can now collect my wife from the hospital without further obstruction?'

'Of course, of course. Everything is normal again.'

'What about my offer?' Mado said, struggling to sit up in a more comfortable position. Marides came over to help Andrea move him so that the three formed a group in opposition to Mr Lamda who stood by the door, the last of the security police having left.

'You're not serious, Mr Mado?' Mr L said with a laugh that sounded more like a cough.

'As I said earlier on, no one ever laughs at my jokes. However, I do want Colonel Voznitsky and I want him in mint condition.'

'Mr Mado – your Colonel Voznitsky and that young man they've just carried out plotted together to eliminate me and Mr Marides from the scene here in Greece. They blew up Mr Marides' house . . .'

'But Colonel Voznitsky was there with me at the time. He could scarcely plot to blow himself up.'

'That was unforeseen – and naturally unintended. Accidents happen in every plan. But they were going to murder Mr Marides and me. They failed. What would you yourself do if you were in my shoes?'

'I'd take those ridiculous dark glasses off for a start,' Mado said, 'so that my beautiful eyes could be seen. Just because you happen to be the number one torturer and murderer here in Greece, is no reason to go around dressed like a Tonton Macoute nor to take such umbrage when someone does back to you what you've been doing to hundreds of your victims since you crawled into power.'

'That kind of talk will get you nowhere, Mr Mado. In fact it could even be dangerous.'

'Listen, sport, I very nearly lost my life – or at any rate some valuable marbles – a few moments ago. I certainly didn't do it to keep you in blinies. To me there's one word for you and your lot – revolting. However, we needn't go into that just now. I came to this marvellous country of yours to get Colonel Voznitsky and get him I did. Now – how about stopping the process down in your filthy police headquarters and letting me take Colonel Voznitsky away from Greece . . . without reprisals and without any further fuss?'

'Incredible!' Mr Lamda said. 'Simply incredible!'

Andrea had now recovered sufficiently from the shock to enable her to speak without too much shaking and shivering. She straightened up and faced Mr L.

'Why don't you do as Mr Mado suggests?' she said. 'Pick up that phone and stop the brutality before it really begins.'

'I advise you to keep well out of this, Miss Eckersley.'

A slightly tremulous look crossed her face and for a second or two Mado thought this had shut her up. He was wrong.

'On the contrary I'm going to get further in. You're supposed to be a man who understands deals, Mr Lamda, so now here's one from me. You've just killed the guerillas' chief of staff, if that's the way to describe him. But you know – and I know – we all of us know that the movement itself goes on. Tomorrow another Nikos will be found. You and your associates will again be under threat. In the end you'll have civil war here as you had it after the second world war – as we have it in Ulster.'

'There will be no civil war because nobody wants it. As

in Spain, Miss Eckersley, one civil war is enough. The Greek people demand a peaceful and prosperous life. We give it them. We know what we are doing. We also know when foreign agitators get into the act and that's when we take the necessary precautions.'

'Mr Lamda or Lycopoulos or whatever your name is,' Andrea said imperiously, 'I've just seen you kill one man and send another to be tortured. The Sunday after I get back to England your life story – with full documentation – will be published by my paper.'

Mr L appeared to be quite unmoved.

'I am already the arch devil so far as the British press is concerned. I can stand another attack. Are you sure you have the documentation you talk about?'

'Oh! yes.'

'I think you may find it missing when you next look through your papers, Miss Eckersley. And your paper might find a libel suit very expensive.'

'My duplicates are already in a bank in London,' Andrea said, without turning a hair. 'The story itself won't take me long to write up.'

'If you get back to London yourself, that is.'

Now it was Andrea's turn to surprise the Greek with a short contemptuous laugh: 'I don't think you'll touch me, Mr Lycopoulos. Herr Entdecken wouldn't like it at all – and then you'd have an unwelcome interruption in your essential supplies, in the one market where you really clean up.'

A silence followed on the mention of Herr Entdecken's name. It meant nothing to Mado but then he knew little of the international drug scene. Herr Entdecken evidently carried a lot of weight with Mr L. Marides, who had been watching this exchange with growing impatience, now took charge.

'You're both wasting time trying to blackmail each other. I suggest you turn over Colonel Voznitsky to the British as Mr Mado has asked and Miss Eckersley will write something else for her paper on her return to London.'

Mr L turned his dark glasses on the Greek millionaire and for a while said nothing.

'Provided there's a cash adjustment,' he said in the end.

'No,' Marides said firmly, 'no cash adjustment. You've got your million Swiss francs for my niece, who has now decided that love conquers even Siberia. Any cash adjustment from now on comes from the other direction. And don't threaten me – or my businesses here in Greece,' he went on before Mr Lamda could open his mouth. 'If I have any more provocation from you and your associates, I pack it all up overnight – and I never come back. You'll be left with some valuable hardware but that's about all. Greece and I have done very well for and with each other. I think your friends would want that state of affairs to continue as it is.'

No one spoke and no one moved. Mado found his eyes returning to the spot where Nikos had fallen to the floor. He was heartily sick of it all. No matter what Padstow might offer, he would never take another assignment like this again. His thoughts went back over all they had been through in the last couple of weeks. To be within sight of success and now to find the result at the mercy of some kind of macabre auction – in which all could be lost if their bid did not succeed – struck him as cruelly ironic.

'Very well,' Mr Lycopoulos said, opening the door, 'enough is enough.' He nodded at Mado and at Andrea. 'I want you both out of the country by midnight tonight. You will write nothing about me in your paper, Miss Eckersley, and Colonel Voznitsky will be delivered to the British Embassy in an hour's time. Of course,' he added as he went through the door, 'since in Greece everyone is free to do as they like, your Russian Colonel may not wish to defect after all – and as you pointed out, he has diplomatic immunity . . . so it will be up to him, will it not?'

After the door had closed behind Mr L there was a lengthy pause while each of them thought out what had just been agreed and what was now likely to happen.

'Thanks, Pan,' Mado said, 'it all depended on you.'

Marides looked at him and unexpectedly smiled.

'I'll get Doctor Spiro to examine your leg. Next time, George, you'll be working for me.'

'Hm!' Mado said, 'you're not supposed to take advantage of a wounded man.'

'Will that creature do as he says?' Andrea asked. Marides nodded abruptly.

'He is totally corrupt. He enjoys both money and power. He'll honour the deal. And so must you,' he added with a sudden warning note in his voice and a sharp look at Andrea. The enigmatic smile had gone from his face and he was again the tough, hard man the world understood him to be.

'It's too good a story to lose,' Andrea pleaded, 'what am I going to tell my editor?'

'However, lose it you will – or you may find Herr Entdecken getting nasty with *you*.'

'You mean it?' Andrea said, playing it unexpectedly soft.

'Ask George whether I mean what I say – and what happens when people don't toe the line.'

Then, without allowing her to comment, he went on sharply: 'I'm now going to collect Elissa and the children. I'll have the 707 ready for six o'clock tonight. We'll be in London by ten. You can tell Mr Padstow he can bring his new Russian friend if he wants . . . and I shall expect a knighthood in due course.'

191

He walked to the door. 'I must find out who they'll be sending as the next Resident to Greece.'

'Why not Ivan Karai?'

'Why not indeed?' Marides said, 'it's an ideal piece of casting.'